Dear Reader,

I just wanted to tell you how delighted I am that my publisher has decided to reprint so many of my earlier books. Some of them have not been available for a while, and amongst them there are titles that have often been requested.

I can't remember a time when I haven't written, although it was not until my daughter was born that I felt confident enough to attempt to get anything published. With my husband's encouragement, my first book was accepted, and since then there have been over 130 more.

Not that the thrill of having a book published gets any less. I still feel the same excitement when a new manuscript is accepted. But it's you, my readers, to whom I owe so much. Your support—and particularly your letters—give me so much pleasure.

I hope you enjoy this collection of some of my favorite novels.

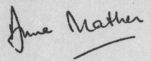

D0720476

Back by Popular Demand

With a phenomenal one hundred and thirty-five books published by Harlequin, Anne Mather is one of the world's most popular romance authors. Harlequin is proud to bring back many of these highly sought-after novels in a special Collector's Edition.

Anne MATHER

COLLECTOR'S EDITION

A TRIAL MARRIAGE

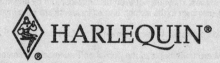

HARLEQUIN®

TORONTO • NEW YORK • LONDON
AMSTERDAM • PARIS • SYDNEY • HAMBURG
STOCKHOLM • ATHENS • TOKYO • MILAN • MADRID
PRAGUE • WARSAW • BUDAPEST • AUCKLAND

ISBN 0-373-63143-X

A TRIAL MARRIAGE

First North American Publication 1977.

Visit us at www.eHarlequin.com

Printed in U.S.A.

CHAPTER ONE

JAKE COURTENAY stood at the long windows of his first floor suite in the Tor Court Hotel, staring out broodingly over the harbour. In the height of summer, the quay was a hive of activity, with fishing smacks and pleasure boats and sailing craft all vying for space in the crowded inner harbour. But in November most of the sailing boats were shrouded with tarpaulin, and although a few hardy yachtsmen braved the autumn gales, most of their owners had packed up and gone away for the winter.

Jake's mouth turned down at the corners. Who could blame them? Torquay in November was no seething Mecca of entertainment, and certainly had the choice been left to him, he would not have chosen this hotel. Of course, he could have stayed at the Boscombe Court in Bournemouth, or the Helford Court in Falmouth, or even the Fistral Court in Newquay, but they were all pretty much the same at this time of the year. His own choice veered more towards the Parkway Court in New York, or the Boulevard Court in Paris, and if he had to have sea air, then the Court Méditerranée in Cannes or the Court Italia in Juan les Pins was more to his taste.

But the choice had not been his. The specialist's advice had been more than eloquent. Indeed, his words had been more in the nature of a dictate than an opinion. Complete rest for at least six months—no work, no travel, no business meetings, no hectic social gatherings, no alcohol—no *stress*.

Maxwell Francis was a friend, of course, as well as a

very successful consultant to the rich and famous. He was used to high-powered business men, who lived on their nerves, and fed their ulcers with champagne and caviare. He was used to treating heart complaints and nervous disorders, brought on by the pressure of living always one step ahead of the rest.

The bite of it all was, Jake had never expected to need him. He had always felt a certain amount of contempt for people who cracked up under the strain. And he had always enjoyed his life. The tensions he had suffered had been quickly dispersed by the next obstacle in his path, and he had deliberately ignored the warning signals his overtaxed body was giving him. The string of Court Hotels was growing every year, and their reputation for good food and good service was the envy of his rivals in the field. His father's dream had been realised, and the national reputation Charles Courtenay had handed on had been expanded by his son into an international one.

But owning hotels in all the major countries of the world required an immense amount of travelling, of entertaining, of sleeping on planes when he could no longer hold back the exhaustion that gripped him. He began to lose weight, he was drinking too much and eating too little, and inevitably the strain took its toll.

Even then he had fought against it. Sitting in business meetings, listening to his executives outlining their plans for the following year, he had suffered agonies over a loss of concentration, an inability to keep his mind on what was being discussed. Where once his head had been seething with ideas, every now and then a curious blankness invaded his brain, so that all he could hear was the pounding of his own heart, and the table in front of him ducked and curved like a rolling ship at sea.

Maxwell had been perfectly understanding, but right

from the beginning he had been adamant. If Jake didn't slow up the pace of his living, he would kill himself. Strong words, particularly to a man who for all the forty-one years of his life had prided himself on his fitness. And naturally Jake hadn't believed him; not then. Time enough to take a break when the Pearman deal was through, when the string of Pearman hotels had been added to the Court organisation.

It hadn't worked out like that. For the first time in his life, Jake found himself unable to control the workings of his own brain. It was rather a case of the flesh being willing and the spirit being weak. That small, rather ugly mass of tissue inside his skull gave up the race and Jake found himself the victim of the disease he had so long despised.

He wondered when the pace of living had first begun to tell. When his marriage to Denise broke up, perhaps? And yet, even in those days, he had been working too hard. One of the reasons Denise had given for the irre-trievable breakdown of their relationship had been his obsession for work, although she had been more than willing to enjoy the fruits of his labours. But she liked the high life, and when his work took him away from the jet-flight capitals she preferred, she had had few scru-ples about finding some other man to share her charms—and her bed.

Jake had been philosophical about her indiscretions. His own life was not so blameless at that time, and if Denise required that kind of stimulation, she could hardly object if he required the same. Until some obscure Italian prince came along and offered her his title as well as his fortune. The idea of being Princess Denise had appealed to her, and she had been able to overlook the fact that her Italian was at least forty years older than she was, and hardly able to stand the pace she set.

But that was Denise's problem. For Jake's part, he scarcely noticed her passing. Their association had drifted so far from any conventional marriage that he had mentally breathed a sigh of relief to be free again. It was a blessing they had had no children. But again, Denise had not wanted them, and although Jake had known his parents had been disappointed that he had not produced a son to follow in his footsteps, he himself knew how much a child of their marriage might have suffered. Nevertheless, after that, he had shared no lasting relationship with any woman. His work had filled his days—and his nights, as well.

And now he was here. A guest in one of his own hotels, identified to nobody except the hotel manager, Carl Yates, who was a personal acquaintance. This had been Maxwell's idea, too, and he had to admit the consultant knew what he was doing. No one would look for Jake Courtenay here, and after that spell in the nursing home he had needed time to humanise himself again. The sense of panic which had epitomised the start of his illness had practically disappeared, but he knew, deep inside him, that the idea of returning to London and the hectic life he had led was still a terrifying prospect.

He drew his hands out of the pockets of the brown corded pants he was wearing and looked at them. The narrow bones showed through the brown skin, but they no longer trembled as they had before. With a sigh of impatience, he thrust them back into his pockets again, and moved away from the window.

It was late afternoon, and already lights were appearing across the harbour. It would be dark soon, and another long evening stretched ahead of him. His eyes flickered over the large square cabinet containing a colour television.

Television, he thought contemptuously. He was sick of television. In the past months he had watched everything from *Coronation Street* to *The Book Programme*, from *Crossroads* to *Match of the Day*. Everything except the news. That had been Maxwell's stipulation. Avoid current affairs programmes and the news...

Jake's face twisted bitterly. My God, he was like a child again, protected from anything which might upset or disturb him. To think he had come to this! Jake Courtenay—mental reject!

A knock at the door provided a momentary respite, but at his command only a waiter entered the room propelling a tea trolley. His afternoon refreshment! Jake pulled a note out of his pocket and handed it to the man with his thanks, although the idea of sitting here alone, drinking tea, was anathema to him. He had been here too long already and he was bored. Bored! A good sign perhaps, and yet anything more strenuous might have him weak and shaking in next to no time. It was galling!

The door closed behind the waiter and with a feeling of futility, Jake seated himself beside the trolley and uninterestedly helped himself to a cucumber sandwich. His appetite was still persistently absent, and food was no more than a rather annoying necessity to living. Living! An ironic humour curled his thin lips. Was this living? Or just *existing*? And what was at the end of it? Would he ever retrieve that enthusiasm for his work which had motivated his life? Without it, he was only half a man.

He rose from his chair again and went back to the window, a tall, rather gaunt figure in the close-fitting dark pants that moulded his lean hips, and a tawny-brown sweater. Strands of silky-smooth dark hair overlapped his collar at the back, liberally streaked with grey. These past few months had laid their mark upon him, and he knew that no one would mistake his age at present as they had done in the past. There were lines etched beside his mouth and nose which had not been there before, and his eyes seemed sunken into his skull. Yet for all that, he was a man who would always attract women, and the hooded depths of dark eyes still proved an irresistible lure.

Along the parade, several shoppers struggled towards the bus ranks, and the light from shop windows spread out across the harbour. There were cars streaming towards the outskirts of the town and Paignton beyond, the curve of the headland a mass of winking lights. His own car languished in the hotel garage, only to be used on very rare occasions. Driving, like everything else he enjoyed, had become a strain.

The grounds fronting the hotel were not extensive. A low stone wall divided them from the promenade beyond, and within the circle the wall provided a few stout palms spread their leaves among less exotic specimens of greenery. Floodlights had been installed among the shrubs so that in summer the Tor Court could hold its own with the other hotels that flaunted themselves after dark in a welter of coloured lights. But during the winter they went unused—except at Christmas.

Looking down, Jake had a first-rate view of the entrance, and as he desultorily scanned the road, he observed two of the other guests returning to the hotel. They were two women—one about his own age, or possibly a little older, the other much younger.

He knew their names. Carl had told him who was staying in the hotel when he first arrived. They were a Mrs Faulkner-Stewart and her companion, Miss Lesley.

Jake had seen them a couple of times already, in the hall of the hotel, and once in the restaurant, although mostly Jake took his meals in his own suite. However, now and then, he felt the need for companionship, and on those occasions he made his way to the restaurant, and suffered the agonies of feeling himself observed by a dozen pairs of curious eyes. That those occasions had so far been rare bore out Maxwell's theory that any kind of mental stress would automatically retard his ultimate recovery.

Watching the two women now, although one of them could scarcely be termed as such, entering the gates brought a latent stirring of curiosity. The girl, she couldn't be more than sixteen or seventeen, he guessed, seemed young to be the companion of a woman of Mrs Faulkner-Stewart's age, and he wondered at her apparent acceptance of the life she was leading. There were no young people of her age staying in the hotel, and the little he had seen of Mrs Faulkner-Stewart had not given him the impression that she was the most patient of women. But the girl seemed happy enough, and had even smiled at him in a friendly fashion in the lobby of the hotel when she passed him on her way out to exercise her employer's poodle. Tall, and not too slim, with long chestnut-coloured hair which was inclined to curl at the tips, she could have no shortage of boy-friends, he mused, yet she seemed perfectly content to pander to the whims of a woman more than old enough to be her mother.

He realised his tea was getting cold and turned back to the trolley with wry impatience at his thoughts. What on earth did it matter to him if some young female found running around after a middle-aged harridan better than doing a worthwhile job of work? It was nothing to do

with him. Besides, judging by the amount of jewellery
Mrs Faulkner-Stewart wore, and the expensiveness of
her furs, she could obviously afford the best of everything, and probably the girl took her for every penny she
could make. The only inconsistent factor was why she
had chosen to winter at the Tor Court instead of in
Cannes or Madeira, or any one of a dozen other fash-
ionable locations.

By the time he had finished his tea it was dark outside,
and on impulse, he decided to go for a walk. At least
that was one pastime which had not been denied to him,
but he obediently put on his thick, fur-lined duffel coat
before leaving the room. The cold was something else
he had to guard against, although he refused to put on
the marathon-length woollen muffler his mother had cro-
cheted for him.

The lift took him down to the lobby where Carl was
standing, talking to his receptionist. The manager lifted
his hand in greeting, but Jake had no desire to get involved in conversation with him and with a brief acknowledgement, strode towards the revolving doors. His
hand had reached out to propel them forward when he
became aware of the girl who had been occupying his
thoughts earlier approaching over the soft grey carpet,
pulled along by the enthusiastic efforts of her employer's
black poodle.

He paused, and the second's hesitation was enough to
create a situation where it would have been rude of him
to barge ahead without acknowledging her presence. He
guessed she would use the baggage door to let the dog
out, and with a feeling of compulsion, propelled it open
and waited for her to pass through.

Anticipating his intention, she had quickened her step,
and her shoulder brushed the toggles of his coat as she

said a breathy: 'Thanks!' passing him to emerge into the cool, slightly frosty air. In a waist-length leather jerkin and dusty pink slim pants she seemed hopelessly under-dressed for the weather, but Jake inwardly chided himself for his concern. She was young—and *healthy*; an enviable condition!

He had expected she would go ahead, and was half disconcerted to find her waiting for him outside, firmly reproving the animal for misbehaving. She looked up and smiled when he came slowly down the steps to join her, and an illogical feeling of unease swept over him.

'It's a cold evening, isn't it?' she commented, short-ening the dog's lead, and falling into step beside him, and Jake was obliged to answer her.

'Very cold,' he agreed, a little stiffly, and she glanced sideways at him, obviously speculating about him, as he had about her earlier.

'How long are you staying at the hotel?' she asked, and he felt a momentary impatience with her curiosity.

'Not much longer,' he replied shortly, and halted, go-ing behind her to cross the road. 'I'm going this way,' he added. 'Good evening.'

The girl stopped beside him, however, and looked obligingly up and down the road. 'I'm crossing, too,' she told him, and he wondered if she knew how much he wanted to get away from her. He was angry with himself for getting into such a position, but angrier still with her for trying to pick him up like this. Had no one ever troubled to explain the facts of life to her? Didn't she realise the potential dangers inherent in attaching oneself to men about whom she knew absolutely noth-ing? She was young, but she was not a child, he thought, irritably aware of the firm breasts outlined against the thin jerkin. Unless she was more knowledgeable than he knew. His lips tightened. This was one alternative, but somehow he didn't care to draw those conclusions. Besides, girls these days had different sets of values.

The wide pavement edging the foreshore gave him plenty of scope to put a comfortable distance between them, but after releasing the dog she seemed quite content to stride along beside him, matching her steps to his, albeit with some effort.

'You're Mr Allan, aren't you?' she asked after a moment, and the alien designation fell strangely on his ears. Allan was his middle name—James Allan Courtenay— and it had seemed a good idea to use that and avoid possible recognition. But it still gave him a moment's pause. He wondered how she knew his name, and decided he would have a few harsh words to say to Carl Yates the next time he saw him.

Now he merely nodded, pressing his hands more deeply down into the pockets of his duffel coat, and she supplied the answer to his unspoken question without even being aware of doing so.

'Della—Mrs Faulkner-Stewart, that is—asked the receptionist who you were,' she exclaimed casually. 'Della always likes to know the names of the other guests. I hope you don't mind.'

Jake glanced at her then, and the humorous mobility of her wide mouth inspired the distinct impression that she knew very well that he did mind. But he refused to justify her amusement by admitting the fact.

'It's no secret,' he said abruptly, and she shrugged, tucking her cold hands into the slip pockets of her jerkin. The wind was tugging at her hair, however, and every now and then she had to lift a hand and push it back from her eyes and mouth. Strands blew against the sleeve of his coat, and their brightness irritated him.

For a few minutes they walked in silence, and then she spoke again: 'My name's Rachel—Rachel Lesley. I work for Mrs Faulkner-Stewart.'

Jake drew a deep breath, but made no comment, and all at once he was aware of a stiffening in her. Perhaps she was getting the message at last, he thought ruthlessly, and was totally unprepared for her attack when it came.

'You're not very polite, are you?' she inquired, with cool audacity. 'Why don't you just tell me to get lost, if that's the way you feel?'

Her words stopped Jake in his tracks, and he turned to stare at her angrily. 'I beg your pardon?'

'You heard what I said,' she insisted, and he saw that the eyes turned belligerently up to his were flecked with amber, like her hair. 'If you want to be alone, why not say so?'

Jake's hands balled themselves into fists in his pockets. 'I see no reason to state what must be patently obvious!' he declared cuttingly, and her lips pursed indignantly.

'I was only trying to be friendly!' she retorted, and his lips curled contemptuously.

'I suggest that—Mrs Faulkner-Stewart, if that is your employer's name, ought to pay attention to her employee's education, instead of probing into other people's affairs! Then perhaps you'd know better than to go around picking up strange men!'

The girl gasped. 'I do not go around picking up strange men! I felt—sorry for you, that's all!'

Jake's reaction to this was violent. That this girl, this *child*—for she was little more—should feel sorry for *him*! Didn't she know who he was? Had she no conception to whom she was speaking?

But of course she hadn't. So far as she was concerned, he was plain Mr Allan, and to her he must present a very different figure from the image he had previously taken for granted. This realisation was strangely reassuring, and in spite of his lingering impatience, his anger was dispersing.

'I'm sorry,' he said at last, with something approaching apology in his voice. 'I—well, I've been out of touch with humanity for some time, and I seem to have lost the habit of civility.'

Immediately the girl's face was transformed, and a wide smile gave it a beauty he had not previously observed. 'That's all right,' she said, without rancour. 'I guessed you'd been ill. You don't look the usual kind of man who would choose to stay at the Tor Court at this time of the year.'

Jake wondered how to answer that. 'No?' he probed, with irony. Then: 'I suppose not.'

The poodle provided a welcome diversion at that moment, making a noisy attack at a snapping Pekinese who was being dragged out of its way by its irate owner. The girl exclaimed: 'Oh, glory!' and darted forward to rescue the poodle's collar, and her laughing apology to the red-faced woman in charge of the Pekinese brought an unwilling deprecation from her lips. Jake watched the exchange with reluctant admiration, and then realised he was wasting a perfectly good opportunity to make his departure. Curiously enough he was less eager to leave now, but the remembrance of what the girl had said still rankled, and ridiculous though it was he resented the feeling of being the object of anyone's pity. That was something he could do without.

Even so, he couldn't resist a glance over his shoulder as he walked away between the cultivated borders, and felt a moment's regret when he saw she had turned back towards the hotel. But only a moment's. She was a nice kid, and probably he had judged her too harshly—after all, nowadays young people seemed to have few inhibitions about anything, and she had only been friendly, as she said—but it wasn't in his interests to become too friendly with anyone at the hotel. No matter how nice people were, they always wanted to know everything about you, and that was something Jake wanted to avoid. Besides, he could imagine Mrs Faulkner-Stewart's reactions if she thought her companion was becoming friendly with a man of his age. No matter how innocent an association might be, someone could always put the wrong interpretation upon it. He could almost see the headlines in the newspapers now: *Middle-aged tycoon takes rest cure with schoolgirl*! God, he shuddered to think of it. The poodle had provided him with a lucky escape, and in future he would ensure that his walks did not coincide with exercising the dog.

CHAPTER TWO

RACHEL DID NOT see him again for several days.

Even though she took to lingering for a few minutes in the lobby before taking Minstrel out for his evening walk, there was never any sign of the tall, dark man whose haggard features had begun to haunt her dreams. He never appeared at mealtimes, and in spite of Della's attempts to draw the manager into conversation, Mr Yates seemed curiously loath to discuss the occupant of the first floor suite.

Rachel didn't altogether understand her own interest in him. After all, he had shown in no uncertain manner that he did not welcome companionship, and he obviously regarded her as something of a nuisance in spite of his reluctant apology. But for all that, she had not mentioned their encounter to Della, and squeezed a small measure of comfort from the knowledge that her employer had not even spoken to him.

Her employer! Rachel grimaced at the thought, as she steered Della Faulkner-Stewart's Mini into the parking area outside the hotel. Six months ago she would never have considered such an occupation, but circumstances could change so many things. Six months ago she had been dreaming of going to Oxford, of getting her degree. Until her father had contracted polio and died all in the space of three weeks, and her mother, dazed after so little sleep, had crashed her car into level crossing gates just as a train was passing. At least, that was the coroner's verdict, though Rachel herself suspected that she had not wanted to go on living. She had been an only child, and she had always known her presence had never really been necessary. Her parents were complete unto themselves, and she had been at times a rather annoying encumbrance.

Nevertheless, the dual tragedy had left her stunned, and the solicitors' subsequent information that apart from a couple of insurance policies, which would provide sufficient funds to pay all outstanding debts, she was penniless, had left her curiously unmoved.

That was when Della Faulkner-Stewart had taken over. She had been a school friend of Rachel's mother's, and although they had not seen her for some years, she had arrived in Nottingham for Mr Lesley's funeral. That she was still in town when Mrs Lesley also died was, she said, a blessing, and she had insisted that Rachel should not attempt her final examinations at such a time. There was no hurry, she said. She herself needed a companion—her previous companion had taken the unforgivable step of getting married—and why didn't Rachel come and live with her for a while? They could help one another.

In her numbed state, Rachel was only too willing to let someone else take responsibility for her. It wasn't until some weeks afterwards, when she found herself at Della's constant beck and call, that she began to appreciate what she had forfeited. But still, she had a little money of her own, and until she could afford to take her finals, she was persuaded that she could be a lot worse off.

Della's husband was dead, too, and sometimes Rachel wondered whether that was why she had come to Nottingham in the first place. Perhaps she had hoped to persuade Rachel's mother to take over the position as her

companion, but Mrs Lesley had been too grief-stricken
at that time to consider it. The truth was, Della was not
the most considerate of employers, and although her husband had left her comfortably placed, she resented being
without a man to care for her. Consequently, she spent
little time at her London home, preferring to live in hotels, always in the hope of finding some man to take her
late husband's place. Her only stipulation was that he
should be English. She despised Europeans, and seldom
went abroad, preferring wholesome British food to what
she termed as 'foreign muck'.

Yet, for all that, Rachel was not actively unhappy. On
the contrary, she was naturally a pleasant-natured girl,
and apart from an occasional yearning for dreaming
spires, she lived quite contentedly, prepared to wait another year or two before striking out on her own.

Now, she pulled the Mini into its space, calmed the
excitable poodle behind her, and opened her door. As
she stepped out into the cool afternoon air, it was starting
to rain, and she reached for Minstrel's lead before allowing him to get out and possibly decorate her navy slacks
with muddy paw marks. There was a strange car parked
alongside the Mini, one which she had not seen before,
and she studied its elegant lines before turning and walking towards the hotel. As she neared the entrance two
men came out of the hotel, talking together, and her
pulses quickened alarmingly when she recognised Mr
Allan and another man.

That he had recognised her, too, there was no doubt,
but she sensed his reluctance to acknowledge the fact.
However, short of cutting her dead, there was nothing
else he could do, and his lips curved in the semblance
of a polite smile, while his eyes looked right through
her. She wondered if he knew how that look affected

her, and how her palms moistened when he said quietly: 'Hello!'

Rachel restrained an eagerness to respond, and replied lightly: 'Hello, Mr Allan. How are you?'

'I'm fine, thank you.'

He cast a challenging look at the older man beside him, as if daring him to contradict the statement, and Rachel's gaze flicked over his companion. There was a resemblance between them, and she wondered if this was his father.

But clearly she was not to be introduced, and before she could think of anything else to say, the two men had passed her. She looked after them, biting her lips, and then entered the hotel ill-humouredly, mentally chastising herself for her foolishness.

What did she expect from him anyway? He was easily as old as her father had been when he died, and he regarded her as little more than a schoolgirl, obviously. Just because he evoked her sympathies...

But no. That wasn't strictly truthful. He had the most incredibly sexy eyes, and in spite of his haggard appearance, he aroused the most wanton thoughts inside her. His attraction for her owed little to whatever illness had brought him here, and she knew that Della would have a fit if she guessed the fantasies Rachel was nurturing. But they were only fantasies, she told herself severely, dragging Minstrel into the lift after her, and showing an unusual lack of sympathy when she accidently stepped on his paw.

Della's suite of rooms was on the second floor. She had reserved a lounge and a double room with bath for herself, as well as a single room for Rachel. Rachel was obliged to use the bathroom on that floor which served two other rooms as well as her own, but she didn't mind.

She invariably took her bath in the evening, while everyone else was in the bar enjoying pre-dinner drinks, and unlike Della she had felt little desire to mix with her fellow guests—until now.

When she and Minstrel entered the suite, Della called peevishly from the bedroom: 'Rachel, is that you?' And when the girl showed her face at the bedroom door: 'You've been a long time.'

Della had had one of her headaches when Rachel went out. They were a persistent torment to her, she declared, although they came in very useful on occasion, when she wanted rid of Rachel for the afternoon.

Now, however, she levered herself up on the quilted counterpane, looking suitably wan in her lacy pink negligee. She was forty-three, and spent half her life trying to look younger, with the inevitable result of achieving the opposite. Her fine hair had been tinted so often that it looked like dried straw until it had been combed into its usual style, and her skin was paper-thin and veined from too much food and too little exercise. She treated Rachel with a mixture of envy and irritation, and disliked feeling at a disadvantage with anybody.

Now Rachel held on desperately to Minstrel's lead, as he viewed the tempting expanse of soft cream carpet spread out before him, and explained: 'I couldn't find that particular brand of cream anywhere. I think Mr Holland must make it up for you.'

The frown which had momentarily creased Della's brow cleared. 'Oh, yes, dear, perhaps you're right,' she agreed complacently, relaxing back against the pillows. 'He does tend to make a fuss of me, doesn't he?'

Rachel reserved judgment, and struggling with the poodle asked: 'Have you had tea?'

'No.' Della shook her head. 'I've just been resting here since you went out.'

Belatedly, Rachel asked if she was feeling better, averting her eyes from the lurid jacket of the paperback novel that unexpectedly appeared beneath Della's flowing skirts.

'A little,' her employer conceded reluctantly, quickly tucking the book out of sight, and Rachel turned away to hide her amusement, saying: 'I'll just give Minstrel a drink.'

'Yes, and ring for tea, will you, dear?' called Della after her. 'I'll be out directly.'

The door was closed and Minstrel offered a glum yelp. But since the disastrous occasion a few days ago, when he had cleared his mistress's dressing table of a large collection of cosmetic jars and bottles, he had not been welcome in her room.

Rachel got Minstrel's dish and filled it from the hand basin in her room. The dog drank thirstily, and through its noisy gulps she rang room service. Afterwards, she wandered over to the windows, looking out rather absently. She wondered when she would see Mr Allan again, or indeed if! How long was he staying? And where was his wife? A man like him was bound to be married, but why wasn't she with him if he had been ill?

The arrival of the tea, and Della's subsequent emergence from her room, left little room for further speculation on the matter, and it was not until she was lying in her bath later that evening that Rachel allowed her mind to drift back to the afternoon's encounter. What did he really think of her? Did he think of her at all? Or was she just a rather annoying adolescent in his eyes? Perhaps he thought she was oversexed and provocative!

Rachel reached for the sponge, and began soaping it liberally. Perhaps she was, she thought irritably. But she had never been troubled with such ideas before.

The usual arrangement was that Della went down to the cocktail bar before dinner and shared in the casual conversation of her fellow guests, while Rachel tidied the suite, fed Minstrel, and had her bath. Then, later, they would meet up **ag**ain in the restaurant and share a table for dinner. After dinner, a few of the guests made up a four for bridge, and as Della enjoyed cards she was invariably included. That was Rachel's cue to do as she liked, but this usually comprised a walk with Minstrel, followed by television and bed, in that order. Occasionally she had agreed to a date with a member of the hotel staff; but these were few and far between, preferring as she did the comparative luxury of reading in her own room, briefly free of Della's fads and fancies.

This evening, however, Rachel felt restless, and after spending longer over her toilette than she normally did, she was late for dinner. She had hesitated a long while over what she should wear. After discarding the chemise dress she had planned to wear in favour of velvet pants and an embroidered smock, she had eventually returned to her original choice, deciding she was being silly in imagining it mattered either way. The chemise was long and made of white sprigged cotton, a ribbon tie beneath her breasts accentuating their fullness; but it was definitely not the sort of dress an older woman would wear, and that was why Rachel had hesitated over wearing it. But she was not an older woman, and there was no use wishing she was.

The lift seemed grindingly slow as it descended to the lower floors, and Rachel was biting her lips impatiently when it stopped at the first landing. Then she stepped back nervously, her cheeks darkening with hot colour when she saw the man waiting to get into the lift. His own expression was less easy to define, but after only a moment's hesitation he stepped inside, joining her in the suddenly overpoweringly confined atmosphere of the square cubicle. In a navy suede suit and a matching shirt, the heavy duffel coat overall, he reduced the proportions of the lift alarmingly, and she was stiflingly conscious of the masculine odour he emanated. Her breasts rose and fell rapidly in her agitation, the nipples visibly hardening beneath the sprigged cotton.

If he was aware of her excitement, he gave no indication of the fact, and his polite: 'Good evening!' was as impersonal as ever. But she had not been this close to him before, and she could see a muscle jerking beneath the shaven beard shadowing his jawline. Perhaps he was not as indifferent to her as he would have her believe, or was it nerves that caused that betraying spasm?

Then, as if impatient with the way she was watching him, he looked at her, and that straight uncompromising stare turned her knees to jelly. It was as well the skirt of her gown covered her legs, or their quivering infirmity would have been visible to his gaze.

'I—are you going down to dinner?' she stammered, needing the release of conversation, but he shook his head with wry impatience.

'I've had dinner,' he told her flatly, and her arms slid round her waist in an instinctively defensive gesture.

'I'm late,' she volunteered, and then the lift had reached the ground floor, and the doors were rolling back.

He stood back to allow her to precede him, and she went ahead jerkily, wishing she wasn't always at a disadvantage with him. If only she had had Minstrel with her, she might have stood a chance of going with him, wherever he was going. But that was purely wishful thinking.

He followed her out of the lift, and then, as if aware of her thoughts, he said: 'No dog today?'

'No.' Her smile was fleeting.

His mouth curled. 'I like your dress.'

The colour in her cheeks deepened again. 'Thank you.'

His lips twitched, and then, as if regretting the impulse to compliment her, he turned away. 'Enjoy your dinner.'

Rachel watched him cross the lobby and disappear through the revolving doors with clenched frustration. Now why had he said that? Did he really like her dress, or was he feeling sorry for her now? Whatever! He had gone, and she had to go and face Della's undoubted irritation because she was late.

But as she crossed the lobby towards the restaurant, Carl Yates' voice hailed her. The young manager of the Tor Court would stir a few hearts himself, she thought inconsequently, although she herself didn't go for husky Vikings with shoulder-length blond hair.

'Oh, Miss Lesley,' he said now, his roving eyes revealing a deepening interest. 'Mrs Faulkner-Stewart asked me to get her tickets for the concert at the Conservatory.' He waved a white envelope. 'Will you give them to her?'

'Thank you.'

Rachel took the envelope, wondering why he had chosen to give her the tickets. Normally he used bell-hops to run his messages for him, and he must know that Della was always to be found taking dinner at this time.

'You're looking particularly attractive this evening,

Miss Lesley,' he continued, with the assurance of a man not accustomed to being rebuffed. 'I didn't know you knew Jake—Allan.'

Rachel's smile was forced. 'I'll give Mrs Faulkner-Stewart the tickets,' she said, and gained a certain malicious satisfaction from his chagrin as she sauntered into the restaurant.

Della had not waited for her. She was already halfway through her smoked salmon, and she took the envelope Rachel proffered with unconcealed annoyance.

'I don't pay you to loiter about in hotel lobbies, Rachel!' she stated, in audible tones, and Rachel couldn't help reflecting, as she reached for an olive, that pride always came before a fall.

Even so, as she lay in bed that night, she found herself reliving those moments in the lift. So—his name was Jake. At least she could thank Carl Yates for that small piece of information. Jake Allan? Yes, she liked it. It suited him.

During the following days, Rachel had little time to herself. Della took to her bed with a stomach disorder the morning following the encounter in the lift, and her fretful demands kept her companion on her toes. There was not even the evening bridge sessions to break the monotony, and apart from those occasions when she managed to slip out of the hotel on the pretext of exercising Minstrel, Rachel was kept busy. She told herself that it was just as well, that time would put things into a better perspective, but the truth was she grew more and more anxious to see him as each day passed. She even began to worry about him, wondering if he had been taken ill again, and whether anyone was looking after him. But there was no one she could ask, apart from Carl Yates, and she had no desire to alert him to her interest. So she ran Della's errands, read to her when she felt like it, looked after Minstrel, and generally made herself useful, trying, not very successfully, to enjoy her life as she had always managed to do.

Towards the end of the week Della was sufficiently recovered to come down for dinner, and Rachel, who had become used to taking her meals in her room, dressed for dinner with some trepidation. What if *he* was in the restaurant? Would he have noticed her long absence? Hardly likely, as he seldom ate in the restaurant anyway. But if he was feeling better...

She wore the chemise dress deliberately. It was flattering, she decided, and with her hair loose about her bare shoulders, she could hold her own—at least, with other girls of her own age.

But Jake Allan was not dining in the restaurant. The table he occasionally occupied was vacant, and the absence of cutlery indicated that it was not about to be used. Rachel's lips compressed disappointedly, and Della, unusually alert after her period of isolation, narrowed mascaraed lids.

'What's the matter?' she asked, glancing round curiously. 'Is the Colonel trying to attract your attention again? He really is the most impossible old roué! I shall have a word with Mr Yates—'

'Oh, please!' Rachel shook her head nervously. 'The Colonel isn't even looking this way! I—I was just thinking that's all.'

'What about?' Della looked suspicious.

'Nothing much.' Rachel managed to distract her attention by opening the menu. 'Oh, look! They've got your favourite food here. Tournedos! They must have known you'd be feeling better this evening.'

When the meal was over, the elderly Colonel Della

had been grumbling about earlier approached their table. He subjected Rachel's cleavage to minute inspection, and then turning to Della exclaimed gallantly: 'Good to see you back, my dear. Game hasn't been the same without you! You will be joining us this evening, I hope.'

Della's indignation melted beneath such outright flattery.

'I've missed our little get-togethers, too, Colonel,' she assured him coyly. 'And I know it's no fun playing with three and a dummy hand.'

The Colonel's wicked old eyes flickered over Rachel again. Then he turned his attention to what Della was saying: 'What? Oh, yes. Well, as a matter of fact, dear lady, we managed to persuade one of the other guests to join us yesterday evening. You've probably seen him around. A Mr Allan.'

Rachel managed to control the start the Colonel's words had given her, and concentrated on her hands curled tightly together in her lap, as Della answered: 'Mr *Allan*!' Her interest was evident. 'Oh, yes. I know who you mean, Colonel. But...' She paused, obviously searching for words to disguise her real feelings. 'He seems such a—quiet man. Always keeping himself to himself.'

'Yes.' The Colonel was losing interest in the conversation. 'So you'll be joining us later?'

'Of course.' Della moistened her upper lip. 'Will—er—will Mr Allan be joining us this evening?'

The Colonel shook his head, and unable to catch Rachel's attention, started to move away. 'Shouldn't think so. Only played because I bullied him into it. See you later, dear lady.'

After the Colonel had gone, Della made a little sound of excitement. 'Imagine that! Him playing cards. It's interesting to know he's not as unapproachable as he appears. Isn't it?' Rachel didn't answer. 'Isn't it?' she repeated.

Rachel forced herself to look up, but all she could think was that last night, when she had passed through the lobby on her way out to take Minstrel for his walk, Jake Allan had been only a dozen yards away, in the lounge, playing *bridge*! It was infuriating!

'You—you seem very concerned,' she said at last, biting back her own frustration.

Della sighed irritably. 'Well, why not? He is the most interesting man in the hotel, after all!'

Rachel licked her lips. 'Do you think so?'

'Of course. Don't you? Oh no, of course you wouldn't. He's much too old for you. Carl Yates is more your scene. I'm surprised you don't make any overtures there. He's obviously more than willing.'

Rachel flushed, as much for what Della had said about Jake Allan as her remarks concerning Carl Yates. But happily her employer only saw what she wanted to see, and right now she was no doubt plotting how she could corner her quarry, and invite him into her circle.

After several cups of coffee, Della left her to go and join her cronies, and Rachel walked disconsolately across the hall. A large television was playing away to itself in the viewing room, but she preferred the smaller set in her room to its huge impersonality. Further along was the bar where residents mixed with casual customers, but the idea of entering its smoky atmosphere did not appeal to her either.

She was on the point of turning towards the lift when Carl Yates came strolling towards her from the reception area. Seemingly unabashed by her unwelcoming frown, he said: 'All alone?'

Rachel gave him a cool stare. 'It certainly looks like it, doesn't it?'

He moved his head in silent acknowledgement of the barb. 'I gather you're not a bridge fanatic.'

'No.'

Rachel would have gone past him, but he spoke again: 'Can I buy you a drink?'

She halted, and turned to look at him. 'No, thanks.'

'Why not?'

She hesitated, tempted to brush him off without a second thought, but out of the corner of her eye she suddenly saw that Jake Allan had just entered the hotel and was crossing the lobby towards them. If she walked away now, he would no doubt stop to speak to the manager, and she would have no opportunity of speaking to him herself.

'I—er—I don't drink,' she averred, mentally measuring the narrowing distance between herself and Jake Allan.

'I'll buy you a tomato, juice, then,' suggested Carl eagerly, but before she could reply a shadow fell across them. Carl turned half impatiently, to see who dared to interrupt them, but quickly schooled his features when he recognised the man. Rachel was impressed. Whoever Jake Allan was, he certainly had the power to bring Carl to attention.

'Good evening,' he said, his dark gaze flickering over Rachel with ruthless detachment. 'Good evening, Carl.'

Carl nodded and smiled, shifting rather awkwardly. 'Did you enjoy your walk, Mr Allan?'

Mr Allan! Rachel raised her dark eyebrows. What had happened to the casual use of the man's Christian name?

'Very much,' Jake Allan was saying now, with a slight upward lift of his mouth. 'Is dinner over?'

Carl nodded. 'Oh, yes. Some minutes ago. Er—the game's begun.'

'Good.' Jake's dark eyes shifted to Rachel again. 'How are you, Miss Lesley? I haven't seen you about the hotel for some days.'

Rachel's knees resumed their unsteady wobbling. 'I—Mrs Faulkner-Stewart has been—indisposed. I've been taking care of her.'

'Very well, I'm sure,' he conceded with faint mockery. He flicked an assessing look in Carl's direction, as if summing up the situation. 'Now, if you'll excuse me...'

Rachel cast a dismayed look at Carl, and then, stumbling over the words, exclaimed: 'Are you going upstairs?' And at his nod: 'So am I. Er—goodnight, Mr Yates.'

The young manager's lips tightened, but there was nothing he could do, and Rachel's heart was pounding as she quickened her step to keep up with Jake as he strode towards the lifts. Both lifts were in operation at that moment, and they were forced to wait for one to make the descent to the ground floor. It was an awkward few moments, not relieved when Jake said suddenly: 'You shouldn't have done that.'

Rachel's cheeks burned. 'Done—what?'

Jake gave her an old-fashioned look. 'Yates will get the wrong impression.'

Rachel quivered. 'I'm not worried.'

'Perhaps *I* am.'

She sighed. 'But why?' she implored. 'I was on my way up to my room when he stopped me.'

Jake ran a hand round the back of his neck, and tugged the hair at his nape. He was wearing a leather overcoat this evening, and the wine-coloured fabric accentuated the sallow cast of his skin. His long legs were encased in dark green whipcord, and Rachel had great difficulty in preventing herself from staring at the narrow welt of brown flesh that appeared between his black nylon sweater and the low belt of his pants when he stretched.

The lift arrived, and Rachel preceded him inside. They had it to themselves as before, and Jake pressed the button for the first floor. He didn't look at her as they were borne upward, and it took only seconds to cover the few feet to his landing.

The doors slid open and Jake took a step forward, but while Rachel was contemplating going up to her room and giving in to the tears that were threatening, he stopped and said: 'What do you plan to do for the rest of the evening?'

Rachel swallowed convulsively. 'What do I—why, watch television, I suppose.'

His stare tore her nerves to pieces. 'And if I offered an alternative?'

'Wh—what alternative?'

He sighed, as if becoming impatient with himself as well as her. 'What's your name? Rachel? Rachel—do you know how old I am?'

She shrugged uncertainly. 'Thirty-eight, thirty-nine…'

'I'm forty-one. How about you?'

She shifted from one foot to the other. 'Nearly nineteen.'

'Eighteen!'

'All right. Eighteen.'

He raised his eyes heavenward. 'I must be out of my mind!'

Without another word he stepped out of the lift, and the automatic mechanism set the doors gliding closed.

Unable to prevent herself, Rachel pressed the button to open the doors again, and stepped through them, feeling a sense of inevitability as they closed behind her, and the lift whined away upward.

Jake, who had been striding along the corridor towards his apartments, glanced over his shoulder as he heard the lift depart, and his brow furrowed angrily when he saw Rachel standing there. He halted abruptly and came slowly back to her, his hands deep in the pockets of his coat.

'What do you think you're doing?' he demanded.

Rachel shook her head, unable to voice what she had thought. 'I—I can use the service stairs,' she stammered, and he uttered a word she scarcely understood.

'You'd better go,' he said. 'If anyone sees you on this floor—'

He broke off expressively, and her lips trembled. 'That would never do, would it?' she burst out, unable to prevent the words in her humiliation.

Jake's dark eyes raked her savagely. 'All right, all right,' he snapped. 'If you don't care, why should I?' He spread a mocking hand towards his door. 'Come into my parlour!'

Rachel pressed her lips together. 'Couldn't we—couldn't we have a drink together?'

'I thought I heard you telling Yates you didn't drink?' he countered.

'I don't. Not much, anyway.'

'Nor do I. My—doctor won't allow it.'

This last was said with heavy sarcasm, and she guessed it had not always been so.

'We—we could have a coffee...' she ventured, but he shook his head.

'I think not.'

'Why not?'

'I have no intention of inciting that Draconian guardian of yours by creating gossip of that kind.'

Rachel caught her breath. 'Della's not my guardian. She's my employer. I'm over age. I can do what I like.'

'And what do you like, I wonder?' he demanded grimly. 'Oh, Rachel, why me? Why not Carl—or that handsome wine waiter—or practically anyone, for that matter!'

Rachel took an involuntary step forward. 'You do—like me?'

His lips twisted. 'Yes,' he muttered, 'I like you.'

Turning away, he pulled his keys out of his coat pocket and inserted them in the door to his suite. As he did so, two elderly women came along the corridor towards them, their curiosity sharpening as they recognised Rachel. A quick exchange of glances indicated the direction of their thoughts, and their reproving: 'Good evening, Miss Lesley!' brought the hot colour to her cheeks.

Jake ignored them, pushing open his door and switching on the light just inside. Then he turned, leaned against the frame, waiting until Rachel looked at him again.

'Well?' he said, as her eyes followed the two women's progress to the lift. 'Wouldn't you like to go with them?'

Rachel hesitated only a moment, and then shook her head, walking determinedly towards him, and preceding him into a luxuriously furnished lounge. The door closed behind her, and only then did she feel relief from the disapproving eyes she had felt boring into her back.

CHAPTER THREE

AT LEAST her surroundings were reassuring. This had to be the best suite in the hotel, she thought. Della's rooms were not like this, and the green and gold pattern of the carpet was reflected in the long curtains and matching cushions. A self-coloured hide suite looked soft, and squashily comfortable. There were several small tables, as well as a television, as big as the one downstairs, and the dining table, in the window embrasure, commanded a magnificent view over the lights of the harbour.

While she looked around, assuming an interest in the concealed lighting above the ceiling moulding, Jake took off his overcoat and slung it carelessly over a chair near the door. Then he moved to stand before the huge marble fire-place, obsolete now, since the introduction of central heating. Against its veined beauty his profile had a dark, forbidding quality, and a momentary sense of panic gripped her.

'Regretting it already?' he inquired dryly, and she looked up at him defensively.

'No.'

'Who were those women?'

'Acquaintances of Mrs Faulkner-Stewart,' replied Rachel offhandedly. 'You have a wonderful view—'

'Will they tell her where you are?'

Rachel sighed frustratedly. 'I don't know.'

'You're not worried?'

'*No!*'

He moved his shoulders in a gesture of dismissal, and

36

her eyes were irresistibly drawn to the lean muscularity beneath the fine material. 'If you insist...' he commented carelessly. Then: 'Tell me about Mrs Faulkner-Stewart? Is she some relation of yours?'

'I've told you. She's my employer,' replied Rachel stiffly.

'Only that?' He seemed surprised. 'An unusual occupation for a girl of your age.' He paused. 'And generation.'

Rachel sighed. 'She was a close friend of my mother's. When—when my parents died within a few weeks of one another, Della looked after me.'

'But surely that wasn't what you intended doing with your life,' he probed. 'A girl like you. Had you no ambitions of—an academic nature?'

Rachel nodded. 'As a matter of fact, I was planning to go to university. But—what with Daddy and Mummy dying... Della said it was better to give myself time to get over it.'

'And in so doing provide her with a ready-made companion.'

'It wasn't as callous as that,' she protested. 'Who knows? I might have failed the exams.'

'Do you intend to try again? Next year, for example?'

'Perhaps. If I have enough money.'

'Money.' His echoing of her word was almost a sneer. 'Ah, yes. Everything revolves around money, doesn't it?'

'I wouldn't say that,' she declared indignantly.

'No?'

'No.'

'So you're a romantic, on top of all else,' he drawled sardonically. 'What a novelty!'

Rachel bent her head. 'Do you want rid of me?'

The expletive he uttered made her flinch. 'Such a re-mark does not deserve an answer!' he snapped. 'Come off it, Rachel. You're not dealing with some callow youth who needs that kind of immature invitation!'

'What do you mean?'

'I mean—coyness doesn't suit you!' he retorted coldly, lifting one suede-booted foot to rest on the iron fender surrounding the hearth. 'Like I said before—I must be out of my tiny mind!'

'If—if that's the way you feel...'

Rachel turned abruptly away, her nerves unable to stand any more of this biting double-talk. She had started this; it was up to her to finish it.

But before she had taken a couple of steps, he moved with surprising agility, interposing himself between her and the door, his fingers closing painfully round the soft flesh of her upper arm. She tried to pull away from him, alarmed by the smouldering look in his eyes, but he jerked her back against him, and she felt the hard length of his body against hers. His arms went round her, slid-ing across her flat stomach, propelling her closer, so that for the first time in her life Rachel could feel the throb-bing heat of his desire.

'You have no conception of how I feel,' he protested roughly, bending his head to brush her neck with his tongue.

Rachel's panic began to subside. 'I—I thought you were angry with me,' she stammered.

'I am,' he retorted unsteadily. 'I shouldn't be holding you like this, and you shouldn't be letting me.'

'Why not?' Her mouth was dry, and she moistened her lips as his hands slid up over her rib-cage to cup her breasts.

But she knew. She had read books, and her instincts

warned her that she was playing with fire. Yet she couldn't help herself. She wanted him to hold her, and the thin material of her chemise was no barrier to the way her breasts responded to his touch, swelling and hardening beneath his experienced fingers.

'Oh, Jake…' she breathed chokingly, using his name without thinking, and with a muffled oath, he twisted her round in his arms and covered her mouth with his.

A thousand stars seemed to explode in her head at the touch of his lips, and she clung to him desperately as the room swung giddily about her. She realised with a pang that she had never been kissed before this moment. The boyish embraces she had endured had never felt like this, and the muscled hardness of his thighs made her overwhelmingly aware of what she was inviting.

He released her lips to bury his face in her neck, his hands tangled in her hair, and she realised he was trembling. There was a heady intoxication in the knowledge that she could arouse him in this way, and her hands burrowed beneath his sweater, finding the slightly damp skin of his back. He was so hard and male and virile, and she pressed herself closer against him, delighting in the strength of his legs against hers.

But suddenly, with a stifled oath, Jake set her free, turning away from her violently, raking back his hair with unsteady hands. He put the width of the couch between them, and then turned to look at her through tormented eyes. Rachel was shocked by his pallor, the way his eyes seemed to have sunk further into his head, and she stared at him anxiously as he made an obvious effort to behave normally.

'What is it?' she cried. 'What's wrong?'

Jake made a negative gesture. 'I think you'd better go.'

'Jake—'

He turned his back on her, resting his hands on the mantel above the hearth. 'God, I need a drink!' he muttered. Then: 'Don't make it any harder than it already is, Rachel. Just go!'

'But why? Why? What have I done?' She was confused. 'Are you still angry with me?'

He sighed, casting a contemptuous look in her direction. 'I think you know better than that,' he told her heavily. He straightened, staring up at the hunting scene pictured above the fireplace. 'I suppose I should apologise. But you asked for it.'

Rachel shook her head. 'Jake, don't say things like that!' she implored wretchedly. 'I—well, I'm sorry if I— if I did something wrong, but I've never—'

'That's just it!' he declared savagely. '*You've* never. But *I* have. And I wanted to, but God help me, *I can't*!'

Rachel's face flamed. 'Why—why not? Or—or is that what's wrong with you?'

A faint wave of colour entered his cheeks at her words, and she was horrified at her own audacity in voicing them. 'Is that what you think?' he demanded.

Rachel quivered. 'I don't know, do I?'

He was breathing hard. 'Well,' he ground out harshly, 'not to my knowledge. But I'm not such a swine as to take advantage of a girl young enough to be my daughter!'

Rachel caught her lip between her teeth. 'That's what you say...'

He made a bitter sound, dragging the palms of his hands down over his thighs. 'If you must know, I had a breakdown! I went to pieces. Couldn't work—couldn't sleep!' His lips curled. 'I was a wreck. But not impotent!'

Rachel pressed her palms to her hot cheeks. 'I—I suppose what you're really saying is, I—I'm not very good at it, am I?'

Jake stared at her frustratedly, and the intensity of his stare achieved its usual breath-stopping effect. Then he said flatly: 'All right—no. You're not very good. You're much too inexperienced.'

The callousness of his statement robbed her of what little composure she had left. 'Then—then why pretend it's anything else?' she cried tearfully, and appalled at her lack of self-control, she turned towards the door.

'Rachel!' His tone stopped her, containing as it did a reluctant reassurance. 'Rachel, I am sorry, believe me. But I am too old for you.'

She swung round again, searching his features for some sign of his real feelings. 'You're not old,' she exclaimed.

'I think we both know I am,' he said evenly. 'And what is more, if your employer learns that you've been here, I run the risk of being blacklisted by the management.'

Rachel bent her head, her hair tumbling with unknowing sensuality about her shoulders. 'I don't believe you care what the management think,' she retorted.

He sighed. 'Well, accept that I care what happens to you,' he said.

Her eyes lifted, seeking his. 'Do you?'

'Enough not to want to ruin your life,' he responded crushingly. 'But thank you for the compliment.'

'What compliment?'

He gave her a crooked smile. 'It's good for my morale to know that a beautiful girl wasn't averse to my kissing her.'

'Oh, Jake!'

She took a step towards him, but he shook his head firmly, and she halted again.

'Go to bed, Rachel,' he told her roughly. 'You'll thank me for this one day.'

Rachel didn't answer him. She just stood looking at him with all the hurt fervour of her untried youth, and he flung himself down on to the couch, closing his eyes against the unconscious allure of her.

'Go away, Rachel,' he said, and she had no choice but to obey him.

In her own room again, Rachel paced miserably about the floor. What a disastrous affair it had been! The brief elation she had felt in his arms had quickly evaporated in the aftermath, but although she knew she ought to feel grateful to him for not despoiling her innocence, she didn't feel that way. She ached with the longings he had aroused inside her, and when she closed her eyes she could see nothing but him—his sardonic face, the long narrow fingers, and the lean muscular strength of his body. She would have stayed with him, if he had asked her to, if he had *wanted* her to; she would have been a willing pupil...

She was scarcely conscious of the passage of time, but a spell must have elapsed before Della came knocking at her door. Not knowing at first who it might be, Rachel quickly switched on the television and went to answer it without any of the coolness she would have liked to have possessed. The older woman's probing stare was denigrating.

'You haven't taken Minstrel for his walk,' Della stated accusingly, and Rachel blinked.

'Minstrel?' she echoed dazedly.

'Yes, Minstrel.' Della looked at her suspiciously. 'What's the matter with you?' She looked beyond her into the room. 'Have you been asleep or something? It's half past ten, and Minstrel hasn't had his walk. In consequence, I've had to call room service to come and clean up the mess.'

'Oh, I'm sorry.' Rachel shook her head helplessly. 'I didn't realise it was so late. I—I suppose I must have fallen asleep.' She coloured at the deliberate lie. 'I—I was watching television.'

'Huh!' Fortunately Della was too annoyed to notice the momentary hesitation. 'Well, I don't think it's too much to ask that you remember a dog needs exercising!' she declared. 'You're not exactly worked to death, are you?'

'No. I'm sorry.' Rachel really was, not least because the last thing she wanted now was a row with Della. 'It won't happen again.'

'See that it doesn't!'

Without even saying goodnight, Della marched away, every generous curve of her over-indulged body quivering with indignation.

Rachel closed the door again and breathed a deep sigh. She knew Della well enough to know that she had not heard the last of the matter. Her carelessness and lack of gratitude would be brought up on every occasion until her employer was satisfied that she was dutifully repentant.

Rachel didn't sleep well, which was hardly surprising in the circumstances. Her over-stimulated body would not let her rest, and Della's angry remarks had not in any way relieved her. Then a warm wind sprang up towards dawn which made the presence of the heating system almost unbearable.

At eight o'clock, she was up and dressed, and letting herself into Della's suite she retrieved the excitable poodle for an early outing. Minstrel showed his gratitude by smothering her in wet doggy kisses, the abrasive lick of his tongue a balm to her troubled spirit.

The sea-front was almost deserted and as the tide was out, she went down on to the damp sand, letting Minstrel off his leash to chase madly after gulls and sandpipers searching among the debris of seaweed on the shoreline. The wind was mild, blowing as it did from the south-west, and she breathed deeply, feeling its riotous fingers through her hair.

Back at the hotel, Della was preparing to go down for breakfast. She viewed Minstrel's sandy paws without enthusiasm, and said: 'Don't let him loose in here. The management apparently take a dim view of clearing up after animals.'

Accepting the implied criticism for what it was, Rachel pushed Minstrel into the bathroom and closed the door. 'I have said I'm sorry, Della. About last night, I mean. I—I don't know how I forgot the time.'

'No, well, nor do I,' remarked Della severely. 'However...I'm going down for breakfast. Are you coming?'

Aware of Della's reproving regard for her appearance, Rachel shook her head.

'I'll tidy up first,' she said, and satisfied, Della left her to go downstairs.

When Rachel entered the dining room some fifteen minutes later, Della was wading through scrambled eggs and bacon. Rachel knew her employer preferred to start the meal without her. That way, Rachel's own choice of grapefruit and toast did not jar so obviously with Della's more liberal demands. She seated herself at the table and by the time her grapefruit had been consumed they were ready to start on the toast together.

Buttering the bread, Rachel could not prevent her

thoughts from dwelling on what Jake might be doing at this moment. Ever since she got up, she had determinedly put all thoughts of him out of her mind, but now, with Della's mouth briefly silenced by food, she was unable to halt the flow of emotion that engulfed her. She went over again what he had said in minute detail, wondering about the illness which had sent him here, wondering why she felt this increasing attraction towards a man who was, as he had said, undoubtedly too old for her.

She crunched impatiently at her toast, returning the Colonel's impudent stare with less animosity than usual, and earning herself a wink from that quarter. She looked away irritably, annoyed that he should imagine she was interested in him, and Della caught the angry tightening of her lips.

'What's the matter with you this morning?' she inquired, pouring herself more coffee. 'Just because I had to chastise you about Minstrel, there's no reason to get huffy.'

'I'm not—huffy.' Rachel reached for her own coffee cup, and then almost choked on its contents when the two women she and Jake had encountered on his landing the night before entered the dining room and approached their table.

Della watched her with evident impatience, and then smiled disarmingly as the two women stopped beside her. 'Good morning,' she said, and indicated Rachel's discomfort with a casual wave of her hand. 'These young people! They're always in such a hurry.'

They both regarded Rachel without sympathy, and she wished she could dissolve into the floorboards at their feet. Then one of them said:

'Did you have a good game last evening, Della? I

heard that you and Colonel Jameson made quite a killing.'

Della flushed with pleasure. 'Well—not exactly,' she demurred modestly. 'But we did do rather well.'

'Yes.' The other woman's eyes flickered over Rachel, recovered now and watching the interchange warily. 'What a pity your companion doesn't play cards. We might make up another table with Mr Allan.'

Rachel's hands clenched together in her lap as Della said: 'I didn't know he played until the Colonel mentioned it. But he seems to keep very much to himself, doesn't he?'

The two women exchanged a glance and Rachel waited for the explosion their revelations would ignite. But instead of exposing her, they agreed with Della, and then excused themselves to move to their own table.

Rachel breathed a silent sigh of relief, but Della's next words were hardly reassuring:

'I'm thinking of giving a small dinner party tomorrow evening, Rachel. Just myself and the Colonel, and one or two others. I wonder if Mr Allan would care to join us?'

The rest of the morning passed in a rather one-sided discussion of whether Mr Yates would allow Della to use one of the smaller reception rooms for her dinner party. She got rather excited at the prospect of presiding over her own dinner table again, and it was as well that she was too absorbed with her own plans to notice Rachel's white features.

During the afternoon, Rachel escaped from the hotel and made her own way to the dunes, some distance from the town itself. She would have welcomed Minstrel's company, but for once Della had decided she would exercise the poodle, and had given Rachel permission to do what she liked for the afternoon. Perhaps she had seen Jake taking his solitary walks, Rachel speculated miserably. Perhaps Della hoped she might encounter him while she was out with the poodle.

It was colder now, and although the chill air was refreshing, Rachel was shivering by the time she boarded the bus back to town. She remained in her seat long after the bus had stopped at the harbour station and eventually the conductor came along the aisle to ask her whether she was feeling well.

'What?' Rachel stared at him without comprehension for a moment, and then realisation dawned. 'Oh—oh, yes. I'm fine. Sorry!'

Colouring hotly, she followed him off the bus, and was aware that his eyes followed her as she hurried along the esplanade towards the hotel. She entered the lobby with her head down, and started violently when a hand closed firmly round her suede-clad arm.

'Rachel!' Jake's low voice was disastrously familiar, and she looked up at him defensively, unconsciously arming herself against his unwelcome attraction. 'Are you all right?'

He was no less disturbing to her peace of mind, and she was frightened by the knowledge that he could do this to her without any apparent self-involvement. She had never before experienced the emotions he could arouse in her, and the desire to throw herself into his arms was as potent as it was foolish. His fingers gripping her arm were painful, but she revelled in the sensation.

'Rachel!' When she made no immediate effort to answer him, he spoke again, glancing impatiently round the lobby, aware that no encounter in such public surroundings went unnoticed. 'Rachel, where have you been?'

'Walking.' She tried to pull herself together. 'I—how are you? It's a cold afternoon, isn't it? My hands are froz—'

'Rachel!' He said her name again as if he couldn't bear this time-wasting small talk between them. 'God, we can't talk here! Come with me! We'll walk along the front.'

But now Rachel found the strength to pull herself away from him, and moving her shoulders in a careless gesture, she said: 'I'm sorry, Mr Allan, I can't stop now. Della will be wondering where I am. I'll see you some other time, I expect—'

'*Rachel!*'

The smouldering darkness of his eyes had its usual effect on her knees, but she forced herself to move away from him, keeping a polite smile glued to her lips. She must not make a fool of herself now, not *here*, and she was very much afraid she might if he said anything more.

The distance to the lift stretched before her like the Gobi desert, but at last she was within the enclosing portals of the small cubicle which would lift her to the comparative safety of her own room. The last thing she saw as the doors closed was Jake standing where she had left him, staring after her, a curiously vulnerable expression on his lean features, and the tears overspilled her eyes.

Fortunately Della was downstairs, taking tea, and only Minstrel was there to share her misery. He was remarkably understanding for once, sensing her unhappiness and nuzzling against her comfortingly.

She managed to make some excuse to Della not to join her for dinner that evening, and had a sandwich brought up to her room. Exercising Minstrel was another matter, but although she looked about her nervously as she crossed the lobby with the poodle, there was no sign of the man who had accosted her earlier. Carl Yates was at the reception desk when she returned, however, and while she wished she could avoid him his undoubted admiration was a salve to her bruised spirit.

'Mrs Faulkner-Stewart has got all her arrangements made for tomorrow evening,' he told her casually, after making the excuse of fondling the animal to hinder her progress. 'That means you'll be free for the evening, doesn't it?'

'I expect so,' Rachel answered cautiously, disentangling the poodle's lead from around her jean-clad legs. 'Stand still, Minstrel!'

Carl straightened. 'I wondered if you'd come out with me,' he murmured, low enough so the girl at the reception desk could not hear him. 'How about it?'

Rachel shook her head. 'I—well, I don't go out much,' she said awkwardly.

'Perhaps you should,' he suggested, his usual assurance daunted. 'You need a change.'

Rachel made an apologetic gesture. 'I'm sorry. I—I'm not sure what Mrs Faulkner-Stewart will want me to do.'

'Then let me know,' remarked Carl at once, seizing on her indecision. 'We could go to a club I know. Have a meal…dance. There's no need to make a booking at this time of the year.'

Rachel wanted to refuse, but something stopped her, and with a half-reassuring smile she left him, walking away towards the lift without giving him chance to say anything more.

Della was waiting for her next morning when she entered the suite to take Minstrel for his pre-breakfast gallop along the beach. It was unusual for the older woman to be up and dressed so spontaneously, but the reason for her eagerness was soon made apparent.

'About tonight's dinner party—' she began, and Rachel resigned herself for a long monologue. 'There'll be eight of us in all. The Colonel, of course, and Mr and Mrs Strange. Then, there's Miss Hardy and Mrs King…'

Rachel tucked her trembling hands into the pockets of her jeans. She scarcely knew the Stranges, who were the second half of the bridge four. An elderly couple, they always seemed engrossed in their game, and paid little attention to anyone who didn't play. But the names of the two women who had seen her with Jake still had the power to send a shiver of apprehension down her spine. Nevertheless, it was Della's next words which caused her the most distress:

'And finally myself…and Mr Allan! Yes,' this as Rachel's lips parted involuntarily, 'he's agreed to join us. Isn't that wonderful? I expect we'll have a bridge tournament later, now that we have eight players.'

Rachel turned away, pretending to search for Minstrel's lead, anything to conceal her tormented expression from Della's probing gaze. How could he, she thought despairingly, *how could he*? And why now? When in the past he had avoided contact with anyone?

'Well?' Della expected some response. 'Haven't you anything to say? Like—congratulations, for example?'

'Congratulations?' Rachel echoed blankly, schooling her features. 'I'm afraid I—'

'You know what a recluse Mr Allan has been,' exclaimed Della irritably. 'Don't you think it's significant that he's agreed to join *my* dinner party?'

'Oh, I see.' Rachel strove for control. 'I—well, yes. You—you've been very fortunate.'

'That's what Miss Hardy said,' remarked Della,

frowning. 'Although I wouldn't have put it exactly like that myself. After all, it's obvious he's a man of the world, well used to the society I can offer. It's natural that as two—sophisticates—in what is without question an unsophisticated gathering, we should have certain things in common.'

Rachel grasped Minstrel's lead like a lifeline. 'You—you could be right,' she managed tightly. 'I gather you won't be—needing me this evening.'

'No. No.' Della could afford to be expansive. 'You go ahead and do whatever you want to do, my dear.' She paused. 'I'll want you to do my hair beforehand, of course, but after that...'

Rachel nodded. 'All right. Now, shall I take Minstrel for his walk?'

Della looked as if she would have liked to say more. She was probably put out by a lack of interest on her part, thought Rachel wearily, but she couldn't pretend an enthusiasm she didn't feel. Her whole being throbbed with indignation at this deliberate attempt on Jake's part to show her the differences between them, not only physically but socially, and she despised herself for still feeling the pain of his betrayal. It was like he had said. They were worlds apart, and no doubt Della would be willing to satisfy him with far more success than she had had.

She half hoped she would see Jake as she took Minstrel out of the hotel, but of course she didn't. The only person she encountered was Carl Yates, and on impulse she did something she would never have done otherwise. She deliberately attracted his attention, and when he came to join her she said:

'Is your offer still open for this evening, Mr Yates?'

'Carl,' he averred. Then: 'You know it is.'

'Good.' Rachel's lips found smiling a difficult task. 'What time shall we leave?'

Carl inclined his head towards her. 'Seven? Seven-thirty?'

'We'd better make it seven-thirty,' she said, remembering Della's hair. 'I'll meet you here, shall I?'

Carl nodded. 'I'll look forward to it.'

Rachel kept her smile in place, and strolled away, with what she hoped was casual assurance, towards the doors, but once outside the cold air against her hot face brought a flush of anxiety to her cheeks. She hoped Carl wouldn't think she was forward. She had never done anything like this before. Somehow, since meeting Jake Allan, she had done a lot of things she had never done before.

CHAPTER FOUR

DELLA DRESSED with extra care for her dinner party. Her gown of oyster pink chiffon floated about her plump figure with a flattering lack of definition, and the jewels that surrounded her neck, and hung with such vulgarity from her ears and fingers, denoted a richness seldom seen at the Tor Court. Her coiffure must be right, too, and Rachel's fingers were aching by the time she had twisted and coaxed Della's coarse hair into a becoming style.

'You really are getting rather good,' Della complimented her grudgingly when she had finished, turning her head this way and that to view the style from all angles.

Rachel put the brushes and combs away. 'Is that all?' she asked, and Della turned toward her curiously.

'What are you planning on doing this evening? Dining alone in the restaurant, or having something sent up here?'

Rachel shook her head. 'Neither. Actually, I've promised to have dinner with Mr—with Carl Yates,' she stated defiantly, waiting for the reproaches she was sure were to come, but for once Della was disposed to be generous.

'I'm glad,' she said, putting tissues into her evening purse. 'I don't like to think of you spending a lonely evening.'

Rachel thought, rather ungraciously perhaps, that Della had never before concerned herself with how many

53

lonely evenings her companion spent, but obviously her success with Jake Allan had gone to her head. Now she was glad just to escape to her own room and take a hurried shower, refusing to admit, even to herself, that she regretted her defiant impulse to accept Carl's invitation.

She seldom wore pants in the evenings, but she wore them tonight. Black velvet pants, that teamed with a matching waistcoat, over a frilled white organdie blouse. The sleeves of the blouse were full, and she looked, she thought, like some medieval pageboy. Then she turned sideways, and the provocative swell of her breasts and the curving line of her hips dispelled the illusion.

She hadn't an evening coat, but her midi-length suede would do. Carl obviously thought so when he saw her coming out of the lift, and his enthusiasm made up a little for her disappointment in not encountering Jake. She had half expected to see him in the adjoining lounge where Della and her cronies were sharing pre-dinner cocktails, but as yet he had not joined them.

Carl drove a Ford Capri, a sleek-backed car with trim red lines edged with black. It was a sporty-looking vehicle without being too expensive to run, he told her, obviously proud of its brisk turn of speed.

The club he took her to was in the basement of a building at the back of the town, high above the illuminated waterfront. An old cellar had been renovated without stealing any of its atmosphere, and the music which was provided by a four-piece group on a raised section of the stone floor, echoed hollowly between stone walls and wooden pillars. The dancing was all modern stuff, requiring little in the way of space, which was just as well in the circumstances.

They sat at a wooden table, spread with a checked

cloth, and ate seafood and salad, washed down by cheap white wine. The place wasn't full by any means, but there were a number of other young people present, several of whom knew Carl, and came over to be introduced to his companion.

After an initially shaky start Rachel began to enjoy herself, finding a certain amount of release in the dancing, letting the rhythmic beat of the drums seduce her into a state of near-amnesia. She danced with other boys as well as Carl, and her success helped to drown the unwilling images of Jake talking to Della, holding her hand, touching her lips... A mental block came down when she tried to go any further, and it wasn't just because she had never experienced anything more herself.

'I mustn't be too late,' she told Carl, as the clock crept round to half past ten. 'Della's arranged for one of the porters to let Minstrel out for a while, but she'll expect me to make sure he doesn't get into mischief.'

'Who?' inquired Carl wryly. 'The dog—or the porter?'

Rachel smiled. 'Minstrel, of course.'

'Don't you get sick of running after a woman like her?' he probed, but Rachel knew better than to discuss her employer with a man who was still practically a stranger to her.

'Della's been very good to me,' she told him quietly, and Carl was discreet enough to know that he was wasting his time making those kind of comments.

'Even so,' he persisted, 'you don't get a lot of free time, do you? I mean, it's a seven-days-a-week job really, isn't it?'

'I don't mind,' replied Rachel firmly, and he gave up asking questions.

In spite of her good intentions, it was after eleven-thirty before Rachel got back to the hotel. Some friends of Carl's arrived at the last minute, and they had insisted buying him a drink, although Rachel refused anything but fruit juice. She had had a couple of Martinis in the course of the evening, and she was determined not to add an aching head to her other problems.

She left Carl in the lobby, unutterably relieved when the night porter approached him with a message, thus preventing prolonged goodnights at her door. She thanked him politely for taking her, and because of the situation, Carl was obliged to let her go. But she realised she had been extremely fortunate in avoiding payment for his attentions.

Nevertheless, as the lift rode upward, all her other anxieties came back into focus, and she wondered whether she had been so clever, after all. What was the point of caring about a man who had made it blatantly obvious that to him she was nothing but a child?

As she came out of the lift, she wondered whether she ought to check on Minstrel, but then stifled the thought. It was late. No doubt Della would be in bed by now, and going into the suite might disturb her. If he had made a nuisance of himself, she would learn about it soon enough, and there was little she could do at this time of night.

She passed Della's door and went to her own, inserting her key in the lock, and letting herself into the darkened room. Her hand groped for the light switch, but before she could turn it on another lamp was illuminated beside the bed, and she gasped with momentary fear. Then she saw Jake, seated on the side of her bed apparently waiting for her, and the gasp died in her throat.

Taking advantage of her stunned amazement, he got to his feet and came over to the door, closing it firmly behind her and remaining there beside it while she caught her breath.

'You've been out with Carl Yates,' he said quietly, his tone revealing a subdued anger. 'Where?'

Rachel gathered her composure. 'What's it to you?' she countered jerkily. 'Did you enjoy the dinner party?'

'I asked you a question first,' he retorted, a certain coldness surfacing. 'Why did you go out with Yates? The other evening you couldn't wait to get away from him.'

Rachel moved away from the door and likewise from him. 'I don't have to answer your questions,' she declared tautly. 'I don't know how you got into my room—'

'With a key!' he interspersed.

'—but I wish you would leave.'

'Do you?' He came away from the door, tall and darkly malevolent in a wine-coloured velvet dinner jacket. 'Why? Because you want time to lie and dream about your boyfriend? Because you now see me for what I am?'

'What do you mean?' She swung round then, staring at his haggard features with troubled eyes. He looked so strained, she thought anxiously, aware of emotions she was trying desperately to suppress. 'You—you're the one who made the rules.'

'Rules? What rules?' His fists clenched. 'Don't play games with me, Rachel.'

'I—I'm not playing games,' she protested. 'I—you chose to go to Della's party—'

'Della's party!' He repeated her words contemptuously. 'Damn you, you know I only agreed to join her band of card fanatics because I expected *you* to be there!'

'What?' Rachel stared at him disbelievingly. 'But I don't play cards—'

'How was I to know what your employer had planned? So far as I was concerned, it was a dinner party, nothing else. Naturally I expected you would be there.'

'Oh, Jake…' Rachel's knees gave out on her this time, and she sank down weakly on to the bed, staring up at him helplessly. 'Jake—I thought you'd done it deliberately.'

'Done what?' He came to stare down at her narrowly, his brooding gaze sending shivers down her spine.

'I—why, going to Della's party, of course. She said you had accepted her invitation, and I… I…'

Jake's eyes darkened. 'Is that why you went out with Yates?'

'Yes. Oh, yes!'

'I see.' He turned abruptly. 'That explains it.'

Rachel felt cold suddenly. 'Ex—explains it?' she echoed, as he walked deliberately towards the door. 'Is—is that all you came here for? To find out—why I went out with Carl Yates?'

Jake reached the door and turned, one hand on the handle. 'That's right. I had to know.'

Rachel got to her feet. 'But why?'

Jake bent his head. 'Call it what you like? Pride—curiosity.' He looked up. 'Or good old jealousy. It's all the same.'

'Jake!' She stared at him helplessly. 'Jake—please. Don't go!'

'I have to go,' he said roughly. 'I can't stay here all night.'

'You—you could,' she breathed huskily.

He shook his head slowly. 'No, Rachel. We both

know I can't do that. Besides,' there was irony in his tone, 'I'm not allowed *any* kind of stimulation.'

'Oh, Jake!'

Before he could open the door, she flung herself across the room and wound her arms around his waist, pressing her face to his chest. He was wearing a ruffled silk shirt beneath his dinner jacket, and the lace tickled her nose, but he smelled warm and male and somehow familiar, and she couldn't bear to let him go without letting him know how much she cared about him.

'Rachel!' His hands touched her shoulders reluctantly, pushing her coat down over her arms, lingeringly probing the bones of her throat. 'Rachel, you don't know what you're doing,' he breathed, the words an obvious effort for him, and as she continued to cling to him, she began to feel the effect she was having on him.

'Don't go,' she repeated, lifting her face to his, and he was no longer capable of denying himself the satisfaction of parting her lips with his own.

She was ready for him this time, and her mouth opened shamelessly beneath his as she moved instinctively against him, arching her body to the muscled hardness of his thighs with all the untried sensuality of her nature. The aching longing she had felt for him gave her all the experience she needed, and she let her coat fall unheeded to the floor.

At last Jake managed to draw back sufficiently to rest his forehead against hers, and she could feel the dampness of perspiration beading his brow. There was a film of sweat all over his face, and she touched his cheek anxiously.

'Jake! Are you—'

'I'm all right,' he assured her, rather tersely. 'Just exercising control, that's all.'

'Jake—'

'Rachel, listen to me. This can't go on.'

She dragged back her head to stare at him. 'Wh—what do you mean?' she demanded painfully. 'Why can't it?' She licked her lips, and then went on awkwardly: 'I—we can wait. Until you're better.'

'Oh, Rachel!' Wry humour twisted his mouth. 'You react on me like—amphetamine. But like amphetamine, you could become habit-forming.'

Rachel's brow furrowed. 'I—I don't think I understand—'

'Rachel, the way I feel right now, I could handle anything, any situation! You give me strength—and confidence. You make me feel like a man again.'

'But that's good, isn't it?' she protested.

Jake inclined his head. 'Yes, it's good. Initially. But in the long term, it's—bad!'

'Why?'

Her eyes were wide and innocent, and he cursed himself for letting things get so out of hand. 'Rachel, you're eighteen! All right, I'll admit—I want you. I want to make love to you. I want to sleep with you. I want to wake up mornings and find your head beside mine on the pillow—but it won't do!'

She moved her head confusedly from side to side. 'Why won't it?'

With a stifled oath he released her, turning away to rake his fingers through his hair. 'Rachel, you know nothing about me, about my past, about my way of life.'

'I don't care about your past,' she exclaimed, shaking her head. 'This is what matters—here—and now!'

He swung round on her then, staring at her narrowly. 'Is that what you think? Is that what you really think?

Are you so experienced in these matters that a night spent with me would mean nothing to you?'

Rachel's cheeks flamed. 'No! No, that's not what I mean, and you know it.'

'Then what are you saying?'

Rachel took a deep breath. 'I—I love you, Jake.'

His face changed, anger contorting his lean features. 'You don't love me, Rachel!' he told her ruthlessly. 'You only think you do. If you were honest, you'd admit you feel sorry for me. You see yourself as some kind of lady of charity, dispensing favours to the afflicted!'

'That's not true!'

'What is the truth, then?' he demanded. 'You want me to take what you're offering? Because, believe me, that's what it sounds like to me!'

'Oh, Jake!' Her eyes filled with tears, and rather than let him see her cry, she stumbled to the window, staring out blindly on to the deserted car park. 'I've never felt like this about anyone before. I can't stand it when you're angry with me!'

'Angry with you! My God!' Jake strode across to her, and jerked her savagely into his arms, pressing her back against him, his face buried in the warm hollow of her neck. 'Rachel, I'm a man of forty-one, who has been married and divorced. Until recently, I ran a massive business concern, a chain of hotels, of which this is one of them. I had a breakdown, like I told you, but soon, God help me, I've got to go back to that kind of life.'

'I don't care,' she protested, turning her head to rest her cheek against his chest. 'The kind of life you've led. The—the women you've known. Unless...' Her voice faltered. 'Is—is there someone else?'

'*No*!' His voice thickened. 'But I'm not a boy, Rachel. I can't act like one. Holding you in my arms like this, kissing you—it's not enough. And I'm not fool enough to imagine that anything else would work!'

'Anything else?' She twisted round in his arms to stare at him. 'What do you mean?'

Jake looked down at her passionately, and she was woman enough to realise how narrow was the line between his control and the lack of it. 'We've known each other such a short time—'

'Time has nothing to do with it!' she cried, and he nodded.

'I accept that there is—something—between us,' he agreed, taking a deep breath. 'But how long do you think it would last, exposed to the kind of pressures we would have to cope with?'

Rachel's lips parted. 'Why don't we try it and see?'

'I can't do that!' he muttered violently.

'Why not?' She put up her hand to his cheek. 'Oh, Jake, I'll do anything you want me to do.'

'No!'

Again he let her go, moving away from her, running his hand round the back of his neck. Rachel watched him despairingly, not knowing what to say, how to appeal to him; only knowing that she loved him more than she had ever loved anyone in her whole life.

At last he turned and faced her, and she stiffened nervously at the serious look on his face. 'All right,' he said evenly, 'I'll lay it out for you, shall I?' He thrust his hands deep into the pockets of his velvet jacket. 'As I see it, it's like this; we could live together for a while— only I won't do that to you.' His lips twisted. 'Don't look like that, Rachel. You should be grateful—'

'Gratefull!' she exclaimed bitterly. 'When you know how I feel...'

'Sure, sure.' He nodded heavily. 'Okay. There are other alternatives.'

'What?'

She was suspicious, and he gave a half smile. 'I'll be leaving here soon, but we could see each other again. Say, in six months from now—'

'Six months!'

Her cheeks lost their colour, and his teeth clenched impatiently. 'Rachel, it's the most sensible thing to do. We both need some time to get things into perspective.'

'Don't you mean out of it?' she demanded painfully. 'You know if you leave here. I'll never see you again!'

'That's not necessarily true,' he declared quietly. Then: 'There is one other way.'

'Why don't you suggest paying my way through college?' she cried chokingly. 'As you seem determined to treat me as a schoolgirl!'

'Is that what you want?' he asked grimly.

'No!' She stared at him tearfully. 'You know what I want.' She spread her hands. 'I want you...'

He took an involuntarily step towards her, and then stopped abruptly. 'Very well.' His direct gaze was penetrating. 'We could—get married.' But when she would have rushed to him, he held her off with a warning hand. 'Wait,' he said. 'I mean—on a trial basis.'

Rachel looked uncertain. 'A—trial basis?'

'Yes.' He heaved a sigh. 'Look—as I've just told you, I'll be leaving here within the next couple of weeks. I'm spending Christmas with my parents, and in the New Year I'm expected to take up where I left off. There's no way I can take you with me unless we—well, make it legal. But that doesn't mean I think either of us is ready for marriage.'

'But Jake—'

'That's the deal. Take it or leave it.'

'Jake!' She linked her fingers together tightly. 'Jake, are you saying that—that—'

'I'm saying we get to know one another, Rachel. Really get to know one another, I mean. Then, if it doesn't work out, I can get the thing annulled without you being involved, one way or the other.'

Rachel shook her head disbelievingly. 'But I know how I feel...'

'You think you do.' He sighed. 'Remember, I've been married before. I know the pitfalls. I just don't want you to get hurt, that's all.'

'But—your parents?'

'What about my parents?'

'What will they think?'

'They need never know. They'll be happy enough thinking that I've found someone else I care about. They never liked Denise.'

'Denise?' Rachel felt a ripple of apprehension slide along her spine. 'Was that—your wife's name?'

'Yes.'

Rachel bent her head. 'Did you—did she—why did you split up?'

Jake gave her a wry look. 'You might say it was a mutual agreement.' He paused. 'As it happens, Denise wanted to marry someone else. An Italian prince, actually, a good deal older than she was.' His lips curled, and she guessed what he was thinking. 'Much like yourself,' he added ironically. 'Except that I'm no prince!'

'Jake!' Rachel refused to let him hold her off any longer, and she pushed aside his reluctant guard, reaching up to press her lips to his. 'Oh, Jake, I'll marry you. On whatever terms you say, you know that. But do you honestly think you'll be able to keep me away from you?'

His breathing quickened as her hands found the buttons of his shirt, tugging the expensive material aside to stroke the hair-roughened skin of his chest. There was an intense delight in being this intimate with him, and Jake was not immune to the probing caress of her fingers. He pulled her to him, not kissing her, just holding her closely, and her limbs melted against the hard strength of his body.

'Rachel!' With a groan, he put her away from him, cupping her face between his hands and looking down at her half impatiently. 'This has got to stop,' he insisted gently. 'And I must go. If we've got to face your formidable employer tomorrow, I think we should do it with a clear conscience, don't you?'

'You really mean it,' she breathed.

'Don't you?' For a moment his eyes clouded, but she quickly reassured him:

'Of course I do!' She bit her lower lip nervously. 'I—you won't let Della—I mean, if she gets angry, you won't—nothing will change your mind, will it?'

Jake ran a long finger over her parted lips. 'Only you can change my mind,' he told her softly, and she quivered when she considered the commitment she was making. She loved him, she didn't doubt that for a moment. But for a moment she wondered if that was enough…

Jake turned away and found the handle of her door. 'We'll have breakfast together,' he said. 'Can you manage that?'

'I—well, I usually have breakfast with Della…'

'All right.' He was unperturbed. 'I'll join you. How's that?'

Rachel shrugged her slim shoulders. 'I—I can hardly believe it!'

Jake opened the door. 'Do you want to believe it?'

'Oh, you know I do,' she breathed.

His eyes darkened, dropping for a disturbing moment down the slender length of her body. Then he gave a determined shake of his head, and stepped out into the corridor. Rachel hurried to the door to watch him walk along to the lift, and then stepped back, aghast, as the lift doors opened and Mrs Faulkner-Stewart emerged.

Rachel didn't wait to see what happened. She silently closed her door and leant back against the wall beside it, her hands pressed to her mouth as if to suppress the gasp of dismay that threatened to betray her. She was still standing there when, without warning, the door was propelled open, and Della appeared, trembling with fury.

'You little bitch!' she declared viciously, and slapped Rachel smartly across the face.

Rachel fell back into her room, staring at the older woman as if she had never seen her before, her hand pressed to her burning cheek. 'I—Della—'

Words would not come, and Della advanced further into the room, slamming the door behind her with a complete disregard for other occupants of the floor who might be sleeping.

'You sly little cow!' she continued furiously. 'Pretending you were going out with Carl Yates when all the time you'd planned to meet that Allan man up here!'

'That's not true—'

But Della was too incensed to listen to explanations. 'Well, you can pack your bags. You're leaving!' she announced grimly. 'I refuse to keep you any longer! You're a selfish, ungrateful girl; you've deceived me, Rachel, and I'd never feel I could trust you again!'

'You don't understand,' protested Rachel desperately. 'I—Jake—we—we're going to get married!'

'*What!*'

To say Della looked shocked would have been a vast understatement. Her face convulsed with colour and for an awful moment Rachel thought she was going to have a seizure. But then she went deathly pale, and sank down weakly on to the side of the bed, groping blindly for a tissue. Rachel watched her anxiously, twisting her hands together, and then sinking down on to her knees beside her, looking up into her distraught features.

'Are—are you all right?'

Della stared at her incredulously. 'Did I hear you correctly? You're going to—marry Allan?'

Rachel nodded her head. 'Yes.'

'But how—*when*? You don't know him!'

'I know him well enough,' said Rachel firmly. 'He—he asked me this evening.'

Della shook her head helplessly. 'But how could he? He was playing bridge until about—I don't know—an hour—an hour and a half ago!'

Rachel sought for words, the pain of her cheek a stinging reminder of Della's uncertain temper. 'We—we've known each other for about two weeks,' she ventured slowly. 'I—from the beginning, we were—attracted to one another.'

'But it's ridiculous!' Della was recovering rapidly; Rachel's passivity infuriated her. 'The man's at least twenty-five years older than you are!'

'Twenty-two, actually,' replied Rachel quietly.

'There you are, then! Twenty-two years, Rachel! He's more than old enough to be your father!'

'Age doesn't matter,' insisted Rachel, getting to her feet again. 'We love each other.'

But as she said the words, she wondered if that was strictly true. She had said she loved Jake, but he had only admitted that he *wanted* her! But he must love her, she told herself fiercely. You didn't marry someone unless you loved them.

Seeing the momentary uncertainty in the girl's face, Della too stood up. 'Love!' she said contemptuously. 'What is love but a satiation of the senses? How long do you think that will last once he's grown tired of your immature body?'

Rachel stiffened. 'I don't need your advice, Della. I'm old enough to make my own decisions.'

'Are you? Are you really?' Della sneered. 'My God, you're a fool, Rachel, do you know that? Throwing yourself away on a man who's already lived one life to the full!'

'I know he's been married before, if that's what you mean,' declared Rachel coldly, but Della was unimpressed.

'He's washed up, Rachel. He had a breakdown, and you know what that means to a man of his age. Who'll employ him now?'

'Employ him?' Rachel almost laughed with relief. 'He doesn't need anyone to employ *him*, Della. *He* employs people. Why, he even owns this hotel!'

Della's eyes narrowed. 'He owns this hotel?' she echoed disbelievingly. 'But—' She broke off abruptly, licking her lips. Then when she spoke again, her voice was unnaturally hushed: 'Rachel, you know who owns this hotel, don't you?'

'Yes, I've just told you. Jake does...'

'But you don't know who Jake is, do you?' Della sighed. 'Of course, the "Allan" threw me. That must be a family name or something. Rachel, these hotels are

owned by the Courtenay group. The man you're planning to marry is not Jake Allan—but Jake *Courtenay*!'

'Well...' Rachel shrugged her shoulders, not altogether happy that Jake hadn't told her himself, but confident enough to realise that such a minor discrepancy
was hardly important. 'What of it?'

Della spread her hands. 'My dear child, you can't
marry Jake Courtenay!'

'Why not?'

'Why not?' Della shook her head. 'Good heavens, I
couldn't let you do it.'

'You can't stop me.'

'Rachel, be sensible! The man's a multi-millionaire!
He'll eat you alive! Can you imagine yourself in his
circle? Can you see yourself handling the kind of society
he mixes in? My God, if it wasn't so tragic, I'd find it
amusing!'

Rachel's face felt stiff and set. 'I don't care what you
say, Della. I am going to marry him.'

'But you're too young, Rachel...'

'I'm growing older every minute.'

'So is he!' declared Della coldly, impatience returning. 'For heaven's sake, Rachel, think! It may seem a
good idea now, but what happens in twenty years' time
when you're my age and he's sixty!'

'I hope he'll still love me,' stated Rachel steadily, and
Della uttered an ugly imprecation.

'You're a fool!' she exclaimed angrily. 'What do you
really know about him, after all? A few clandestine
meetings can't have told you a lot, except that he appears
to prefer to keep you out of the limelight.'

'That's not true!' cried Rachel again, refusing to let
her spoil what had been such a marvellous ending to her

evening. 'We—we're having breakfast together tomorrow. He—he *was* going to speak to you then.'

'Really?' Della's lips curled. 'I suppose he told you he was going to ask my permission.'

'We don't need your permission,' repeated Rachel determinedly. 'Della, can't you at least say *one* thing in favour?'

'No.' Della was abrupt. 'I've told you what I think. God knows why he wants you, but he apparently does. You're attractive enough, I suppose, although he must meet dozens of women with more sex appeal than you have. You're young, of course. And hopelessly naïve. I suppose he thinks you'll be easy enough to get rid of when the time comes.'

'Please go, Della.'

Rachel had had enough. It was one thing to defend their discrepancies in age, and quite another to discuss the intimate side of their relationship. That was too private—too new—to bear exposure to Della's particular brand of malice.

'You'll regret this,' remarked Della, but she was moving towards the door as she spoke. Perhaps she realised she had gone far enough, and Rachel's white face bespoke the uncertainty she denied. Whatever, after a pitying stare, the other woman left her, and Rachel wrapped her arms about herself tremblingly, aware that in some way Della had succeeded in pricking her bubble of happiness.

CHAPTER FIVE

JAKE'S CAR WAS A Lamborghini. After Della's revelations Rachel was hardly surprised, but its sleek green lines only served to emphasise the differences between them. Strapped into the safety harness, she viewed the passing countryside with a certain amount of trepidation, that owed nothing to the expert way Jake was handling the powerful machine.

But the day had not started well, and she could not pretend it had. She had slept very badly after the confrontation with Della, and awakened feeling totally incapable of facing the day ahead. Minstrel had still needed his walk, however, and until she actually left Della's employ, she felt obliged to exercise him.

Back at the hotel, Della had been waiting for her, and they went down to breakfast together, an almost unique experience. Rachel half wished she could have avoided this, but short of remaining in her room like the coward she felt herself to be, she was forced to go through with it. And after all, it was what she wanted, wasn't it? Only Della had planted the seeds of uncertainty inside her, and she had no one else to turn to for reassurance.

The dining room had not been busy. There was no sign of Jake, and for a few minutes she had wondered whether she had dreamed everything that had happened the night before. But five minutes later he had appeared, lean and attractive, in an expensively casual suede suit, his bronze roll-necked shirt both a complement and a contrast. Was it her imagination, Rachel wondered, or

71

did he look different this morning, very much the assured and successful businessman he must have been before his illness; or was that only due to Della's influence? Whatever, she found it incredibly difficult to believe that a man of his experience and sophistication should find anything of interest in a nobody like herself, and when he stopped by their table she was almost offhand in her acceptance of his suggestion to join them. It was left to Della to wish him good morning, and his dark gaze flickered only briefly over the girl before moving on to exercise his faultless charm on her employer.

Della, for all her angry disparagement of the night before, behaved as if there was nothing at all unusual in the elusive Mr Allan joining them for breakfast. Not even when the waiter almost performed a double take on seeing him sitting at their table did she show, by so much as a flicker of an eyelid, that she had noticed anything amiss. She ate her breakfast and exchanged small talk with their guest, and not until she was buttering her toast did she say:

'Rachel tells me that you and she—have plans, Mr Allan. Or should I say Mr Courtenay?'

Jake's eyes flickered over Rachel's bent head. She had scarcely exchanged a glance with him throughout the whole meal, and she sensed his simmering impatience. But now she felt the smouldering penetration of his gaze, and the involuntary stiffening which had followed Della's statement.

'I suppose it was too much to hope that you wouldn't have heard of me, Mrs Faulkner-Stewart,' he responded quietly. 'And yes, Rachel and I do have plans. We intend to get married, don't we, Rachel?'

Now she was forced to look at him, and the directness of those glittering eyes was denigrating. 'I—yes,' she agreed tautly, drawing her lower lip between her teeth, and his mouth tightened as he turned back to answer Della's next question:

'Can you give me any idea when you intend making this official?' she inquired, not entirely liking the sensation of being excluded which Jake had achieved when he looked at Rachel. 'I mean, I have to find someone else to take Rachel's place, don't I?'

Rachel almost gasped. Only the night before Della had threatened to throw her out. Now she was behaving as if her departure would cause the most awkward situation.

Jake was unperturbed, however. 'I'm taking Rachel to meet my parents today,' he said, without giving Rachel any choice in the matter, 'and I imagine we'll be married some time within the next two weeks.'

'Two weeks!' Now Della was really shocked. 'You can't mean that!'

In fact, Rachel herself was astounded by this news. *Two weeks!* Did he really intend to make her his wife in two weeks?

'I don't see any point in waiting, Mrs Faulkner-Stewart,' Jake continued implacably. 'Our minds are made up, and after Christmas I may not have the time to spare to give Rachel the attention she deserves. Besides,' he reached for Rachel's hand, and her heart skipped a beat as those hard brown fingers closed round hers, 'we don't want to wait, do we?'

Rachel shook her head, but her expression was hardly encouraging, compounding as it did a mixture of uneasy embarrassment and self-consciousness, and Della's lips thinned. 'Well, I think you're both behaving rather recklessly,' she declared coldly. 'You hardly know one another, and as I feel myself *in loco parentis*, as it were, so far as Rachel is concerned—'

'Rachel is eighteen,' Jake reminded her, equally coldly, and Rachel herself felt obliged to make a contribution:

'I'm going to marry Ja—Mr Courtenay,' she asserted, stiffly. 'I told you that last night, Della.'

After that, there was little more to be said. As soon as breakfast was over, Jake advised Rachel to go and get her coat, and this she did with alacrity, wishing above all things to avoid another confrontation with her employer. But when she came downstairs again Jake was alone in the lobby, and he explained briefly that Della was still in the dining room, probably relating the news to her cronies.

And now they were on their way to meet his parents. He had offered her no further explanations, just installed her in this luxurious vehicle, and made himself comfortable behind the wheel. A *fait accompli*, but Rachel felt as nervous as a teenager on her first date.

As if sensing the troubled train of her thoughts, he spoke at last, shifting his eyes briefly from the road to encounter her anxious gaze. 'My parents live in Somerset, a place called Hardy Lonsdale. I doubt if you'll have heard of it.'

'No.' Rachel shook her head, her eyes darting uneasily over the lapels of his jacket, anywhere rather than hold his curious stare. 'Do—are they expecting us?'

'Yes.' He inclined his head. 'I phoned them first thing this morning. They're looking forward to meeting you.'

Rachel looked down at the green corded pants suit she was wearing, wondering whether she ought to have worn something more formal. Jake's suit wasn't exactly formal, but he had the build and appearance to look good in anything he wore, while she… Her mouth felt parched. Dear God, this time yesterday she had been resigning herself to the fact that he didn't even like her, and now...

'Rachel!' His impatient use of her name brought her face up to his, and she saw the sudden hardening of his jawline. 'What's the matter?'

'N—nothing.' She shook her head again, her hair brushing his shoulder, leaving one gleaming strand clinging to the soft suede. 'I—why should there be?'

'I don't know.' He swore softly. 'But there is.'

With a violent tug on the wheel he pulled the car off the road on to the hard shoulder, and switched off the engine. Then, releasing his harness, he turned abruptly in his seat to look at her.

'Come on,' he said. 'I want to hear it. Is it something your redoubtable employer said? Or the fact that I didn't tell you my real name?'

Rachel unfastened the straps that confined her, primarily because within them she felt trapped, and feeling trapped was the last thing she needed right now.

'I—Della thinks we're mad, of course.' she said, almost stumbling over the words in her haste to get them out. 'But then so will your parents, I suppose, and everyone else we come into contact with.'

Jake's brows ascended. 'Is that what you think?'

'Don't you?'

He studied her troubled face expressionlessly. 'You've changed your mind,' he said flatly. 'I should have expected it.'

Rachel stared at him, her breast heaving with the tumult of her emotions. But she couldn't let him get away with that. 'I haven't changed *my* mind,' she declared tremulously, and he scowled.

'Are you suggesting *I* have?'

'I—why, no. Not exactly...'

'Then what are you saying?'

Her tongue appeared to wet her upper lip, its tentative exploration an unknowing provocation to the man watching her. With a muffled exclamation, he hauled her into his arms, and his mouth imprisoned the moistness she had just created.

'Oh, Rachel!' he breathed, one hand sliding possessively along the curve of her spine. 'Don't do this to me! I can't stand it.'

She was weak with longing for a satisfaction she had not received when he finally let her go, expelling his breath on a heavy sigh, resting his heated forehead against the coolness of the steering wheel. 'Well?' he said at last, turning his head sideways to look at her, and she allowed a faint smile to touch her lips.

'Della—Della made it all seem—impossible somehow,' she confessed, daringly running her own fingers over the muscular hardness of his thigh, and with a wry smile he lifted her hand and dropped it back into her lap.

'Della would,' he said, straightening his spine. 'Does her word mean that much to you?'

'Oh, no!' Rachel curled her legs up beneath her, and knelt there facing him. 'But—what she said, I felt—like a toy. Something amusing to be picked up for a while and then—dropped. Oh, she talked about you being too old for me, too, but that didn't matter. It was—it was you being—who you are.' She made a helpless movement of her shoulders. 'Are you really a millionaire?'

For a moment Jake's mouth hardened. 'Does it matter?' he asked flatly, and she searched awkwardly for words to express her feelings.

'It—it's all so new to me!' she explained. 'I can't take it in. I mean, how will I fit in with the people you know?

I'm not like them. I've never had any money. How much simpler it would have been if you'd been just—Jake Allan!'

'Would it?' His expression grew cynical. 'I wonder how many girls would agree with you.'

'Jake, you don't think—'

Her eyes were wide and indignant, and he quickly shook his head. 'No, I don't think. If I did, do you think we'd be here now?'

Rachel looked solemn. 'Just thinking about the kind of life you lead—it frightens me.'

'It needn't,' he reassured her, his tone gentling. 'But nevertheless, perhaps it will help you to appreciate the sense of what I said last night. We shouldn't—jump the gun. We both need time to adapt, and that's what I intend we should have.'

A provocative smile lifted Rachel's lips. 'What if—what if I can't—satisfy you?' she ventured softly, and with a determined effort Jake swung round in his seat and fastened his safety harness.

'Let's cross that bridge when we come to it, shall we?' he suggested dryly, giving her a sidelong look. 'Even you are not that naïve, Rachel.'

Her cheeks deepened with bewitching colour. 'But I don't want to wait, Jake,' she protested, her arm sliding along the back of his seat, and he was forced to remove it rather brutally before slamming the powerful car into gear.

Hardy Lonsdale was a pretty village, off the beaten track of tourists, and therefore practically unchanged for centuries. White-painted cottages edged the village green where a few hardy ducks waded from the pond, and even on this grey autumn morning it had a charm that appealed to Rachel. Two swinging signs indicated the liquid refreshment establishments of the hamlet, and Jake casually indicated one of these as they drove through.

'Do you want a drink before we meet my parents?' he asked, and she arched her eyebrows questioningly.

'I thought you weren't supposed to.'

'I said you, not me,' he corrected her, half mockingly. Then: 'No, Rachel, I don't need that kind of moral support. I know what I'm doing.'

'Do you?'

She stretched out her hand towards him and he took it in a firm grasp, his thumb probing the sensitive area of her palm. 'Oh, yes,' he insisted softly. 'I know.'

Rachel wished he would stop the car again and take her into his arms. Only there did she feel truly secure. Somehow, just looking at him, she could not believe this man really wanted her.

But he didn't, and needing some kind of contact, she said: 'Is it much further?'

Jake shook his head. 'About a mile, I guess. My father bought the old priory when he retired, and he's had it modernised for his own use.'

'The priory?' Rachel was intrigued. 'Was it really once a priory?'

Jake nodded. 'About two hundred years ago. Since then it's run through a variety of uses—almshouse, riding stables; once I believe it was used as a private school for the sons of gentlemen!'

Rachel looked ahead with enforced eagerness as they left the village behind and turned almost immediately on to a narrow private lane which led to the gates of the priory. But she was nervous, and she couldn't disguise the fact.

'You've seen my father before,' Jake remarked reassuringly, as they drove between iron gateposts and up a rhododendron-lined drive to the house. 'At the hotel. Remember?'

'So you did notice me,' she murmured with an attempt at lightness, and he gave her a lazy smile.

'I noticed,' he agreed dryly. 'Well, here we are!'

The priory still possessed a curious aura of asceticism. Maybe it was in the severe lines of the slate dark walls overhung with creeper, or simply that the cloistered portico was typically monastic in appearance. A gravelled forecourt fronted the building, and Jake parked the Lamborghini here alongside a grey Mercedes, which Rachel had seen before in the car park at the hotel.

Her hands trembled as she undid the safety harness, and she was glad of Jake's helping hand to get out of the car. She cast another doubtful look at her trousers, checking that at least they were uncreased after the two-hour journey, and then accompanied him across to the door of the priory.

She had half expected his parents to come out to meet him, but no one appeared, and he opened the heavy studded door himself, and ushered her into the huge hall. Here the original intention of the building was less obvious. The stone floor was concealed beneath boxed wooden flooring that gleamed with the patina of age, and the rugs strewn about its shining surface were thick and colourful. The fireplace had been maintained, however, and presently logs were burning brightly, dispelling the gloom of the morning. The walls, too, had been lined with wood, but the tapestries which provided decoration were obviously very old. Several high-backed armchairs and a sofa invited relaxation, but Jake led the way across the hall to the carved wooden staircase which wound round two walls to the upper floor.

'The living rooms are up here,' he explained, when

she followed him at his instigation, and then he stopped short as a woman came through the door below the stairs and stood staring up at them. She was small and thin, and rather disapproving in appearance, in her sixties, Rachel estimated, and judging by her apron, a member of the staff.

'Good morning,' she greeted them dourly.

Jake's face relaxed into a reluctant smile. 'Good morning, Dora. Is my mother in the drawing room?'

'No, she's not,' responded Dora, without warmth. 'She and your father are outside. They didn't expect you so early, and Mr Courtenay's mare is foaling.'

'Oh, I see.' He turned, and following his example, Rachel led the way back down to the hall. Standing once more on solid ground, Jake explained: 'This is my old nurse, Dora Pendlebury, Rachel. She and her daughter both live at the priory. Dora looks after the house-keeping and Sheila, that's her daughter, works as my father's secretary.' He paused. 'This is Rachel Lesley, Dora. My—fiancée.'

It was a unique experience, hearing herself described in those terms, and Rachel looked up at him before holding out her hand to the housekeeper. His eyes revealed that he was not unaware of the significance of his words and for a brief moment they shared an intimacy that was almost tangible. But when she turned back to Dora, Rachel surprised a curiously hostile reaction to their close-ness, and a disturbing shiver of apprehension ran down her spine. They shook hands, and the housekeeper offered congratulations, but Rachel knew instinctively that Dora did not like her. She wondered why, and then dismissed the thought as Jake took her hand to guide her outside again.

'Are you warm enough? Do you need your coat?' he

asked, as he closed the door behind them, but Rachel shook her head. The pants suit was warm, and the scarlet jersey she had teamed with it had a polo neck.

He led the way along a path that turned down the side of the building, and reached the stables by way of a kitchen garden where greenhouses bore witness to some-one's horticultural ability. The stable yard was cobbled, and Jake briefly explained that this had once been the bakehouse.

'The ovens are still here,' he said, 'dating back to the eighteenth century, but they are used mostly for storing animal feed these days.'

Rachel knew his words were intended to reassure her, but she was tense as she accompanied him into a barn-like building, smelling of straw and disinfectant. If Dora had been disposed to dislike her without cause, what might she expect from his parents?

Three men and a woman were crowded around the stall where the foaling mare was lying, but the woman turned when she heard their footsteps, and exclaimed delightedly when she saw her son.

'Jake! Darling!' she cried, coming to meet him with out stretched hands. 'You're early! Did Dora tell you where we were?'

Jake released Rachel to take his mother's hands, and while they exchanged greetings she hung back ner-vously, silently admiring the older woman's appearance. Even in these coarse surroundings, Mrs Courtenay man-aged to look coolly elegant, her tweed suit and brogues, a fitting accompaniment to sleekly cropped grey hair and metal-framed spectacles. Rachel guessed she must be in her sixties, and yet she would have put her age nearer the fifty mark.

'You must be Rachel.'

Unobserved, Jake's father had come to join her, and now Rachel turned to him, flustered, realising she had been staring at Jake and his mother to the exclusion of all else.

'I'm sorry,' she apologised awkwardly. 'Yes, I—I'm Rachel.'

Mr Courtenay smiled. He was very like Jake, as she had noticed that day on the car park, but like his wife, his hair was quite grey. 'I've seen you before, haven't I?' he continued easily. 'You were the young lady who spoke to Jake that day I came to visit him.'

'That's right.' Rachel shook the hand he held out to her, but with a grimace, he drew her closer and kissed her cheek.

'As we're going to be related,' he commented, as Jake and his mother came to join them. 'Rachel and I have met,' he added.

'So I see.' Jake's eyes on her were disruptively possessive. Then he drew her forward. 'This is Rachel, Mother. I hope you two are going to be friends.'

Was there a hint of warning in his words? Rachel hadn't time to speculate at that moment because Mrs Courtenay bestowed a light kiss on her cheek before surveying her thoroughly, and saying: 'So you're Rachel! I'm very happy to meet you.'

Rachel sought for words, but things like 'Likewise, I'm sure' and 'Pleased to meet you' kept coming into her head, and she couldn't repeat either of those. So she said: 'Thank you,' and looked imploringly at Jake as if for inspiration. Taking pity on her, he said:

'I expect Rachel's frozen, aren't you? We didn't stop on our way here.'

'You didn't!' Mrs Courtenay clicked her tongue.

'Jake! You know what the doctors said about not over-doing things.'

'Leave him alone, Sarah.' Her husband shook his head in mock disapproval. 'He looks well enough to me.'

'He's too thin,' declared Mrs Courtenay at once. 'Much too thin. Jake, don't they feed you at the hotel?'

'I don't do anything to get hungry,' replied her son good-humouredly. 'How is our Lady?' He nodded towards the mare in the stall, and one of the other men present turned to speak to him.

'She's in a bit of a state, Jake,' he said, and Jake moved towards him, leaving Rachel with his parents.

'That's Sam Gordon,' Mr Courtenay told her. 'He looks after the horses for me, and that chap kneeling down beside the mare is Frank Evans, the local vet.'

Rachel cleared her throat. 'I—is the mare in trouble?' she got out nervously, and Mrs Courtenay sighed.

'She was too old to foal,' she stated impatiently. 'And now it's a breech.'

'She'll be all right,' said her husband doggedly. 'Frank won't let her down.'

To Rachel's surprise, Jake took off his jacket and hung it over the rail beside the vet's, squatting down on his heels beside the mare and running seemingly expert hands over its abdomen. They exchanged a few words on the mare's condition, and after a moment the vet nodded and got up to take a bottle of oil from his case.

'Jake!' His mother hastened to the rail to look down at him with evident concern. 'Come along. We'll go up to the house and have some coffee. Dora's preparing lunch for one, but there's plenty of time.' And when he ignored her, she added sharply: 'Don't go getting involved here, Jake. You're not fit.'

'If you say I'm not fit again, I'll—' Her son broke off

abruptly as the vet handed him the bottle, and he rolled up his shirt-sleeves and began to smear oil over his arms. Then he looked at Rachel. 'You go on up to the house with Mother, darling,' he said, and she quivered at the casual use of the endearment. 'I won't be long.'

'Jake!' His mother was clearly not happy. 'Jake, Mr Evans can manage.'

'No, he can't, and you know Sam can't help him with his back. Go along, Mother. Show Rachel the drawing room. So far, all she's seen is the hall and the stables.'

Mrs Courtenay looked as though she would have protested again, but her husband took hold of her arm and drew her firmly away from the stall. He took Rachel's arm, too, and they all emerged from the stables together.

'Leave him alone,' he told his wife quietly, but with an underlying edge of impatience. 'You know Jake has always been able to handle Lady better than anyone else.'

'But what if he catches cold!' exclaimed Mrs Courtenay worriedly, and Rachel felt the other woman's anxiety communicating itself to her, too.

'He's not a boy, Sarah,' her husband affirmed steadily, and with this she had to be content.

Dora opened the door to them on their return. Rachel guessed she must have been watching for them, and Mrs Courtenay asked for coffee for three before leading the way upstairs.

A central landing ran to the back of the house, with the east and west wings of the building creating a kind of crossroad of passages at the head of the stairs.

'We don't use all the rooms these days,' remarked Jake's mother, as she opened double doors into a magnificently furnished drawing room which was off the central landing. 'Naturally, heating a place of this size is prohibitive, but it's good to know we have the space if we need it.'

'Yes.'

Rachel's interjection was inadequate, but she was staring wide-eyed at the appointments of the room, and it was difficult to think of anything else at that moment. The high ceiling was arched and the original woodwork had been replaced with carved beams. The walls were also framed with wood, and hung with heavy apricot silk that was echoed in cushions and curtains, and the thick soft carpet underfoot. A grand piano stood at one end of the room, and its generous proportions in no way dwarfed a room which could happily accommodate a pair of sofas, at either side of the huge open fireplace. Yet, for all that, it was a lived-in kind of room, with well-stocked bookshelves and magazines strewn on a table near the hearth.

'Everything has to be on the grand scale here,' remarked Mr Courtenay, coming into the room behind Rachel and grinning wryly. 'Could you imagine this room with a conventional three-piece suite and little else? It would be lost.'

Rachel nodded. 'It's beautiful. A marvellous room for a party.'

'That's what we thought,' agreed Mr Courtenay, pulling a pipe out of his jacket pocket and putting it between his teeth. 'We may have the wedding reception here. What do you say?'

'Oh...' Rachel shifted awkwardly from one foot to the other. 'That's very kind of you.'

'Jake tells us your parents are dead,' inserted Mrs Courtenay. 'You're very young to be alone in the world.'

'Yes.' Rachel accepted Jake's father's invitation to sit on the edge of one of the tapestry-covered sofas, and looked up at her future in-laws nervously. 'My parents were only children, and I had no brothers or sisters.'

'You've been staying at the Tor Court, I believe,' went on Mrs Courtenay, ignoring her husband's silent admonition not to probe, and Rachel nodded.

'That's right. I've been working for a friend—a friend of my mother's, that is. I—she was visiting us when my mother died, and she suggested I needed to get away for a while.'

'Away from where?'

'Sarah!' Mr Courtenay sounded disgusted. 'Leave the girl alone, can't you? You're not conducting an interview. Rachel will tell us all about herself in her own good time.'

Mrs Courtenay tightened her lips. 'You're very young,' she declared, giving her husband a resentful look. 'Have you known Jake long?'

'Not long,' Rachel admitted uneasily, wondering if Jake had deliberately left her to face this inquisition alone.

'Long enough,' put in Mr Courtenay in her defence, and she flashed him a grateful smile.

A knock at the doors heralded the arrival of Dora with the coffee. She carried the tray into the room and set it down on the table by the hearth, pushing several of the glossy magazines aside in the process.

'Do you still want to eat at one, Mrs Courtenay?' she asked, and Jake's mother shrugged her shoulders irritably.

'That rather depends on how long Lady takes to foal,' she remarked caustically.

Dora nodded perceptively. 'I'll watch for Jake coming back,' she said, and left the room.

At least the arrival of the coffee necessitated Mrs

Courtenay's sitting down to serve it. She occupied the sofa opposite Rachel, and Mr Courtenay moved to stand with his back to the fire, lighting his pipe with a taper.

Rachel accepted her coffee with cream but no sugar, and then feeling obliged to volunteer some information about herself, said: 'I come from Nottingham, actually. My father was a cost accountant.'

'Did your parents die together?' inquired Mr Courtenay, and somehow his compassion made the question a natural one.

'Not exactly,' Rachel said now. 'My father contracted polio about eight months ago. He died, and my mother— well, she had an accident in her car just a few days later.'

'How awful for you!' Even Mrs Courtenay sounded sympathetic. 'And you're so young!'

'I'm eighteen, actually,' said Rachel steadily, wondering whether Jake had avoided telling his parents this. 'But I know what I'm doing.'

'I'm sure you do,' observed Mrs Courtenay thoughtfully, and Rachel wondered whether she had imagined a certain irony in her tone. Perhaps his mother thought she was marrying Jake for his money. Stranger things had happened, but until last night she had not known he had any money to speak of.

'I love Jake,' she said suddenly, surprising both his parents with her honesty. 'I'll do anything I can to make him happy.'

There were a few moments silence after her words, and then Mrs Courtenay said gently: 'Perhaps you will at that. You know of course that his previous marriage ended in the divorce court.'

'Yes.' Rachel's voice was steady.

'And you know he's been ill.'

'If she didn't already, she would now,' remarked Mr

Courtenay, shaking his head. 'How you do harp on that subject, Sarah.'

'It's only right that Rachel should know all the facts, Charles,' declared his wife severely. 'Jake has been ill, and there's no point evading the issue.'

'Jake overworked!' retorted Mr Courtenay forcefully, and his wife seized on that point at once.

'Exactly,' she said. 'And yet you're still prepared to let him take over Sam's job in the stables the minute he gets home!'

'Of course.' Mr Courtenay was scathing. 'We both know that Jake would have preferred to work with animals, don't we? He enjoys it. But—to please me, and incidentally, you as well—he took over the Courtenay chain, and a damn fine job he's made of it.'

Rachel felt the need to make some contribution, if only to prevent their argument from escalating into something more serious: 'I didn't know Jake was interested in animals,' she said hastily.

Her words halted their interchange as she had hoped they would. 'He wanted to be a vet,' remarked his father, looking wryly at his wife. 'But he's our only son and naturally I wanted him to be a chip off the old block.'

'And Jake has a good business brain,' put in Mrs Courtenay firmly. 'I don't know whether he'd have been content with a country veterinary practice.'

'He never had the chance to find out,' contributed Mr Courtenay, shaking his head. 'But still… That's all old history now.'

'Have you thought about where you're going to live after you're married?' asked Mrs Courtenay, returning to the attack, and Rachel gave an involuntary shiver. Marrying Jake was still such a nebulous event, and considering where they might be going to live seemed such an audacious circumstance.

But luckily, Mr Courtenay again came to her defence. 'There you go again, Sarah,' he said. 'Poking your nose into things that really don't concern you.'

'Oh, *Charles*!'

Mrs Courtenay looked annoyed, but she asked no more questions, and when Jake came into the room Mr Courtenay was engaged in showing Rachel an antique chess set which he had found on a visit to Hong Kong.

Immediately his son appeared, however, Mr Courtenay rose to his feet. 'Well?' he exclaimed, and Jake made a calming gesture with his hands.

'A filly,' he said flatly. 'But they're both alive.'

'A filly!' Rachel saw Mr Courtenay's disappointment. 'All that fuss for another mare!'

Jake's eyes sought Rachel's, and he grinned. 'See the thanks I get,' he remarked mockingly, and his mother nodded indignantly.

'Indeed,' she exclaimed. 'You should be thankful Lady's survived the ordeal!'

Mr Courtenay grimaced and then gave a shamefaced smile. 'Dammit, I wanted a colt,' he muttered. Then he patted his son on the shoulder. 'Thanks anyway, Jake.'

Rachel looked up at her fiancé. The expensive suede suit was stained in places, and his hands had been scrubbed with the disinfectant she had smelt earlier in the stables.

'I know,' he said, dropping down on to the couch beside her. 'I need a bath. I'll get one in a minute, but right now I could surely drink some coffee.'

His mother bustled with the cups, giving Rachel no chance to take charge, and he accepted the coffee from her with a lazily knowledgeable smile.

Rachel felt hopelessly inadequate. What had happened to her natural assurance, her ability to exchange small talk as she had done with the elderly regulars at the hotel? She had never been a particularly shy person, but suddenly she was allowing the overtones of the situation to colour her own personality. Money was not important, she told herself fiercely, but she wasn't convincing.

As if sensing her anxiety, Jake finished his coffee and rose to his feet, a hand on Rachel's wrist pulling her up, too. 'Do you mind if I show Rachel around, Mother?' he inquired, but it was purely a perfunctory question, for he was already crossing the room as he spoke, taking Rachel with him.

'Of course, go ahead.' His father acknowledged the gesture, but his mother had to have her say:

'Lunch is at one,' she warned. 'You've only got half an hour if you want to bathe and change.'

'All right, Mother.' Jake's tone was resigned. 'I'll have Rachel scrub my back if I don't have the time,' and ignoring his fiancée's burning cheeks, he hustled her out the door.

Once outside, however, his expression hardened slightly. 'This way,' he said, and releasing her arm, set off along the corridor leading into the west wing.

The room they entered was obviously his. Apart from the fact that it was excessively masculine in its austerity, wall photographs indicated his various stages of development, and cups occupying the top of a chest of drawers denoted the different sports he had competed in successfully.

Jake viewed the room without enthusiasm, however, and gesturing towards the cups exclaimed unsmilingly: 'My mother insists on keeping those things. You won't find anything like that in my apartment, I assure you.'

Rachel turned from examining the cups with troubled eyes. 'Your mother—your parents care about you, that's all. I think it's—wonderful.'

'Do you?' Jake slung off his jacket, unbuttoning the matching waistcoat with impatient fingers. 'Is that why you looked at me like a drowning man looks at a straw when I came in?'

Rachel tucked her thumbs into the pockets of her jacket, lifting her shoulders awkwardly. 'I—did I do that? I'm sorry. I—we—your father was showing me his—'

'—chess set. Yes, I know.' Jake was abrupt, tugging off his waistcoat and seeking the buttons of his shirt. 'Was it so bad?'

'Bad?' Rachel swallowed convulsively. 'It wasn't bad at all.'

'But you're not comfortable here, are you?'

'I don't know. I—how can you ask that?' She stared at him defensively. 'I'm—nervous, that's all.'

'Why are you nervous?' he demanded, taking off his shirt, and she wondered how far he intended going in her presence.

'Wouldn't you be?' she challenged, trying to keep her eyes away from the brown expanse of flesh he had exposed. There was a gold chain around his neck, she saw, and suspended from it, a tiny gold crucifix. 'You—you knew how—difficult this was going to be for me, but you chose to leave me to it.'

Jake sighed. 'I thought it might be the best way,' he declared. 'After all, you seemed to find speaking to me easy enough in the first instance.'

Rachel's lips parted in hurt indignation. 'That was different, and you know it!' she exclaimed, ignoring the fact that only minutes before she had been thinking along the same lines. 'Anyway,' she added, 'if that's all you brought me here for, I might as well leave you to take your bath!'

Jake tossed the belt of his pants on to the brown patterned bedspread, and stood regarding her grimly, hands pushed into his hip pockets as if to quell the urge to take hold of her.

'Rachel, I'm not trying to start an argument with you, but these people are only my parents. I want you to feel—at home with them, not on edge!'

Rachel held up her head. 'What you're really saying is if I can't get along with your parents, I haven't much chance of getting along with your friends, is that it?'

'No!' He spoke violently. 'That's not what I'm saying at all. I just want you to relax, that's all.'

'And what if I can't?'

He shook his head abruptly, turning away to grip the edge of the dressing table behind him, and anxiety overrode all else. 'Jake!' She was beside him in a moment. 'Are you all right?'

The face he turned towards her was paler than before, and she realised what a strain this was for him, too. 'I guess Lady took more out of me than I thought,' he muttered, his mouth twisting with self-derision. 'Watch this space, Rachel! Be sure you know what you're getting into.'

'Oh, Jake!' She stared up at him appealingly, but he drew back from her obvious invitation.

'I'm sorry if I was brutal,' he said heavily. 'As you can see, even the smallest amount of exertion reduces me to this! Put it down to body fatigue. Obviously I'm not as fit as I thought I was.'

'Jake...' Rachel's nails dug into her palms. 'Do you

honestly think that makes any difference to the way I feel about you?'

His eyes darkened, but he turned away, and walked steadily towards the bathroom. 'Give me five minutes,' he told her softly, 'then I'll show you the rest of the house.'

CHAPTER SIX

HE EMERGED not many minutes outside his estimate in a towelling bathrobe, his hair curling damply from the steam. Watching him from the objectivity of a velvet bedroom chair, a pile of his old university textbooks in her lap, Rachel wondered how she had existed so long without this man in her life. Now she couldn't imagine life without him, and perhaps, in some subconscious corner of her mind, she had always known he was there.

He slid back the doors of the wardrobe and pulled out a brown suede suit, similar to the one he had discarded, together with a shirt and clean underwear. Then, when Rachel's nerve-ends were tingling with anticipation, he opened a second door into what appeared to be a dressing room and went inside.

'Where did you find those old things?' he called, and Rachel sighed.

'From this cupboard beside the bed. Your mother evidently doesn't like throwing things away.'

She heard his attractive laugh, and was tempted to go to the door of the dressing room and see what he would say. But common sense kept her in her seat. She had learned from experience how ruthless he could be in pursuit of his own ideals, and while physically she could arouse him, mentally he was always in control.

He emerged a few seconds later, fastening the buttons of his waistcoat, pulling on his jacket. 'That's better,' he commented, and then catching her eyes upon him, he walked determinedly towards the door. 'Come on,' he said, and his voice had thickened slightly. 'We don't have a lot of time for the mystery tour.'

Jake did not linger long over showing her the bedrooms but concentrated instead on the huge dining room, which could accommodate a score of guests in comfort along the polished refectory table. Velvet-seated dining chairs backed on to long carved serving tables and sideboards where silver candelabra indicated intimate dinners by candlelight.

'We shan't be lunching in here,' Jake added, noting Rachel's awed expression, and she looked relieved. 'There's a small parlour which we use for family occasions.'

'Thank goodness!' Rachel smiled at him in mutual understanding, and then wondered if he was aware what his direct appraisal could do to her. She decided that he probably was. After all, as he had said, he was no boy, and he must have long appreciated his sexual attraction for women.

As well as the dining room there was Mr Courtenay's study, an impressive book-lined room, where Jake confessed he had suffered many a dressing down, and a smaller, less imposing sitting room, with a rack of paperbacks and a colour television.

'Television!' Jake muttered, grimacing. 'I've watched more television in the last three months than I've ever watched before.'

Rachel regarded him sympathetically. 'Will you tell me what it was like—the breakdown, I mean? I'd like to know.'

'Why?' His dark eyebrows quirked. 'So you'll recognise the symptoms if it happens again?'

'No!' Rachel was indignant until she saw him smile

and realised he was only teasing her. 'I just want to share everything with you, that's all.'

'We'll talk about it,' he promised softly, and then it was time to join his parents for lunch.

A young woman was waiting with the Courtenays in the drawing room. Tall, and quite slim, with curly dark hair and conventionally attractive features, she was apparently quite at home here, and although Rachel had a moment's uncertainty, Jake's friendly exclamation of 'Sheila!' confirmed that this was his father's secretary, Dora Pendlebury's daughter.

Jake and Sheila shook hands, and she inquired warmly after his health, while Rachel accepted the glass of sherry Mr Courtenay offered her. Sheila was in her early thirties, Rachel guessed, and instinctively she concluded that she was the reason for the housekeeper's animosity. Maybe Dora had hoped that Jake's second excursion into marriage would take place closer to home, and certainly the way Sheila was looking at him seemed to confirm her supposition.

Then Jake was introducing her to the newcomer, and in spite of a fleeting glimpse of something which might have been dislike in Sheila's eyes, she treated Rachel charmingly, showing none of her mother's dour antagonism.

Although Rachel had expected Sheila was joining them for the meal, she disappeared after toasting them with a glass of sherry, but as Mrs Courtenay led the way into the cosy parlour adjoining, she said, anxiously: 'Your father gave Sheila the day off purposely, and Dora told me she'd gone into Glastonbury. But obviously she decided to come back.'

There was evident regret in her voice at this turn of events, and her husband cast her a reproving look. 'It doesn't matter, Sarah,' he exclaimed, forestalling his son and holding Rachel's chair for her. 'Now, this looks good, doesn't it?'

Rachel was about to agree that the slices of honeydew melon, spiked with glacé cherries, did indeed look delicious, but Mrs Courtenay insisted on having her say.

'I'm sorry, Jake,' she said, turning to her son, who had seated himself opposite Rachel at the circular table and was presently shaking his napkin on to his lap. 'But perhaps it was as well to get it over with.'

Rachel, embarrassed by the obvious meaning behind Mrs Courtenay's remarks, looked down uncomfortably at her plate, and Jake's mouth turned down sardonically at the corners.

'What my mother's trying very heavy-handedly to say,' he said, 'is that Sheila Pendlebury and I have known one another since we were children and when my marriage to Denise broke up, there was a concerted movement among the women here to find someone to console me.' His eyes narrowed as they lingered on Rachel's bent head. 'Unfortunately, Sheila didn't fit the bill.'

'Right,' said his father, with some relief. 'Now we've got that out of the way, perhaps we can get on with our lunch.'

Rachel picked up her fork as Mrs Courtenay said defensively: 'It's as well to make these things open!' and chancing a look at Jake was warmed by the intimate smile he gave her. It had been quite a visit, but she was learning.

After lunch they all adjourned to the drawing room again, and seated on the couch beside Jake, with his arm along the cushions behind her, discussing in general terms their plans for the future, Rachel thought she had never felt more content. It was only as the shadows be-gan invading the corners of the room, and Jake sug-gested it was time they started back, that a little of her earlier uncertainty returned to torment her.

Jake was leaving the hotel at the end of the week. That was one of the things which had been decided, and he would make all the arrangements for their wedding at Hardy Lonsdale parish church in two weeks' time. After the wedding, they would spend Christmas with his parents, as Jake had said, and return to London in the New Year. There was no talk of a honeymoon, but Ra-chel knew that marrying Jake was the important thing, and where they spent their life afterwards didn't matter, so long as they were together. Even so, she dreaded see-ing Della again, and telling her their plans. There were times when she was torn by the terrifying certainty that she was dreaming all this, and only Della's cruel insin-uations were real.

It was dark by the time they got back to the hotel, and Jake was looking distinctly strained. It had been his most strenuous day since the start of his illness, and he asked Rachel if she would mind if he went straight to bed.

Standing with him in the gloomy interior of the un-derground garage, Rachel was concerned by the grey-ness of his features. 'Would you like me to come with you?' she asked, and then realised at once what she had said when Jake gave her an old-fashioned look.

'I know what you mean,' he assured her softly, 'but no. I don't think that's a good idea on either counts. You're too distracting, and I am tired.'

'All right.' They walked across to the lift together, and Rachel tucked her arm possessively through his. 'I'll see you in the morning, hmm?'

'Without a doubt,' Jake agreed, bending his head to press a lingering kiss on her parted lips.

Rachel wished she could go straight to her own room when the lift reached her floor, but of course she had to let Della know she was back, and that necessitated going into her suite instead. Della was dressing for dinner, but she came out of her bedroom when she heard Rachel come in, and regarded the girl maliciously.

'Well?' she challenged. 'Have you had a good day?'

'Lovely, thank you.' Rachel looked about her. 'Where's Minstrel?'

'A lot you care,' jeered Della. 'As a matter of fact, Mr Yates has taken him for a walk.'

'Mr Yates?' Rachel was visibly surprised. 'But—

'He was most interested to hear about your *engagement*!' continued Della coldly. 'But naturally, as he knows your Mr *Allan's* real identity, he wasn't altogether surprised.'

Rachel allowed the barb to go unacknowledged, and turned back to the door. 'If you don't need me any more this evening, Della, I'll—'

'I didn't say that,' inserted Della sharply. 'I want to know what's going on. When are you leaving? Or is that classified information?'

'No.' Rachel held up her head. 'I'm getting married in two weeks. If you want me to, I'll work for you until then.'

'I'm honoured.' Della was derisive. 'Are you sure your—fiancé will permit it?'

'Jake's leaving at the end of this week,' Rachel told her quietly. 'He'll stay with his parents until we're married.'

'How nice!' Della had picked up a jar of foundation cream from her dressing table, but now she slammed it down on to the glass surface again with unnecessary force, her lips moving angrily. 'Well, hear this, Rachel! Don't you come running to me when things start going wrong and expect me to take you back again, because I won't!'

'Oh, Della—'

'Don't "oh, Della" me! I've been good to you, and this is how you repay me!'

Rachel let her go on, wishing there was some way she could have avoided this. If only Della had tried to understand, instead of pretending a martyred outrage over a relationship she had tried to establish for herself.

'Where are you going?'

As Rachel reached for the door handle, the older woman's shrill tones made her turn back. 'I'm going to my room, Della,' she replied carefully. 'There's no point in continuing this. We both know that you don't really feel anything but contempt for me, and last night you were quite prepared to dismiss me out of hand.'

'I should never have gone through with that,' exclaimed Della indignantly. 'Everyone says things they don't mean in moments of stress. I was upset and angry. How else did you expect me to react?'

Rachel heaved a sigh, and determinedly opened the door. 'I'm tired, Della,' she said, tension causing a tight band around her temples. 'I don't want any dinner, but I'll take Minstrel out later on, don't worry.'

Della sniffed, dabbing at her nose with the back of her hand. 'I wonder what your mother would think about you marrying a man more than twenty years your senior,' she demanded.

'I imagine that so long as I was happy, she would be happy, too,' retorted Rachel shortly, and slammed the door behind her.

In her own room, she flung herself on the bed with a feeling of intense restlessness. If only there was someone she could talk to, she thought dejectedly. Some woman who, unlike Della, would understand her feelings for Jake—and her anxieties, too.

In the morning, everything looked different. Two weeks would soon pass, and she couldn't wait to belong to Jake, to be able to call herself his wife and be with him every minute of the day—and night.

Jake did not appear at breakfast time however, and she had to hold herself in check until Della had finished her meal before escaping from the dining room. Even then, she only made it as far as the lobby before Carl Yates caught up with her, and his expression did nothing for her morale.

'I understand you're to be congratulated,' he remarked, an underlying core of bitterness sharpening his tone. 'I believe one usually congratulates the man on these occasions, but I have to hand it to you. You've really pulled off the catch of the season!'

Rachel was in no mood to tolerate anyone's criticism. 'I don't have to stay and listen to your insolence, *Mr* Yates,' she told him scathingly, hot flags of colour burning in her cheeks. 'What I choose to do is my own affair, and just because I allowed you to date me on one far from memorable occasion, it does not give you the right to offer opinions in matters about which you are—happily—ignorant!'

Carl's fair complexion revealed his embarrassment. His previous experiences with Rachel had not prepared him for this articulate virago, and the fact that she was delivering her comments within sight and sound of anybody passing through the lobby of the hotel caused him to glance about him in mortification.

'Rachel!' he groaned weakly. 'For goodness' sake, lower your voice! All right, perhaps I have been a bit hasty, but at least try to understand how I feel. I thought you liked me! That night we went out together, you didn't tell me I was only standing in for Big Daddy!'

A reluctant trace of amusement lifted the corners of Rachel's mouth. Then she shook her head. 'It wasn't like that. And I do like you, Carl. At least, when you're not playing the heavy. We had a good time together, but Jake and I...' She made a helpless gesture. 'I'm sorry.'

Carl was encouraged by her changing attitude. 'I only wanted you to know that I shall miss you,' he explained, making a concerted effort to win her approval. 'I mean...' He possessed himself of one of her hands. 'We were just getting to know one another.'

She was still looking at him abstractedly when the lift doors opened and Jake emerged, and immediately Rachel was conscious of her hand held within Carl's and of how their appearance must seem to an onlooker.

She pulled her hand away from Carl's as Jake strolled across to join them, his expression revealing none of the jealous anger she had nervously expected to see. Carl visibly came to attention as his employer approached, and his polite: 'Good morning!' was at once a greeting and, to Rachel's ears, an unspoken plea for understanding.

'Good morning.' Jake returned the salutation easily, smiling at Rachel and bringing a becoming sparkle to her eyes. He looked much better this morning, she thought with relief, the lines of strain carved the day before ironed out after a night's rest. 'I'm sorry I couldn't join you for breakfast,' he added. 'I overslept.'

'I—er—I understand you and Miss Lesley are going

to get married, sir,' Carl faltered awkwardly. 'Congratulations!'

There was a moment's silence after his words while Jake toyed with the buttons of his leather overcoat and the other sounds of the hotel went on, effectively creating a barrier around them. Rachel felt herself tensing, and her eyes darted anxiously to Jake's.

At last he said: 'Thank you. But I'm sure you don't call my fiancée Miss Lesley any more than I do.'

Carl was taken aback. 'Well, I—'

'Relax.' Jake's tone was laconic. 'I don't expect you to stand on ceremony, Carl. Besides, you've been out with her yourself, haven't you?'

'Just to a disco,' Carl protested, and Jake nodded.

'I know.' He transferred his attention to Rachel. 'Go and get your coat. We'll take a walk.'

'Oh, but...' Rachel glanced meaningfully towards the dining room, and Jake sighed.

'I'll take care of Mrs Faulkner-Stewart,' he assured her, and after another awkward pause Rachel hurried into the lift.

When she came down again, Jake was lounging on one of the maroon leather settees that were set about the reception area, reading a newspaper. He put it down at her approach, however, and rose to his feet.

'Ready?'

'Yes.' Rachel looked up at him anxiously. 'How are you?'

'Well, I've left my cane behind this morning,' he told her gravely, but when she broke into a relieved grin, he remained unsmiling. Rachel's amusement quickly disappeared, and she accompanied him outside feeling chillier than the weather warranted.

'Did—did you speak to Della?' she asked as he strode

along beside her, hands thrust into his coat pockets, defying any attempt on Rachel's part to take hold of his arm.

'Yes, I spoke to her,' he acknowledged levelly. 'She was quite amenable when I explained that I wanted to buy you an engagement ring.'

'Oh, Jake!' Rachel's lips parted to admit an icy blast of air into her mouth, and she gasped with the cold. 'You don't have to do that.'

'Why not?' He halted abruptly, and she went a couple of steps further on before she could control the momentum and come back to him. 'I thought diamonds were a girl's best friend.'

Rachel sighed. 'What I mean is—it's not necessary to buy me another ring. I—I'll be wearing your wedding ring in two weeks.'

Jake tilted his head on one side. 'Have you any idea how diamonds appreciate in value? A ring bought today might be worth two hundred pounds more in a couple of years' time.'

'So what?' Rachel frowned. 'Why are you telling me this? Why should I want to know about the resale value of a diamond ring?'

Jake shrugged. 'I just thought you might be interested Denise sold all her jewellery when she inherited the Perrucci emeralds. I believe she made somewhere in the region of thirty-five thousand pounds!'

Rachel understood now. 'You mean you're only buying me this ring so that I'll have something of value to sell when we split up, is that it?' she demanded.

'You've got the picture,' he agreed tonelessly, and her heart thumped sickeningly in her ears.

'Well, if that's all you're buying it for, forget it!' she declared, controlling the treacherous tremor in her voice.

'Whatever you care to believe, I don't want your money, and you can keep your diamond rings for someone who'll appreciate them!'

Jake stared down at her broodingly. 'Brave words,' he drawled. 'What it is to be young and have ideals!'

Rachel heaved a deep breath. 'We're quarrelling, and there's no need for it,' she exclaimed. 'Just because you came downstairs and found Carl holding my hand—'

'Not just because of that!' he corrected her grimly. 'I've done a lot of thinking since yesterday, and I'm becoming more and more convinced this was a crazy idea!'

'What!' Rachel's knees went weak.

'You heard what I said, Rachel. I have one disastrous marriage behind me. Why should I assume ours would be in any way different, particularly as there are other complications.'

'What other complications?' she cried, turning up her coat collar against the chill wind blowing off the sea, and he regarded her half impatiently.

'Us,' he said flatly. 'You and me. The material differences between us notwithstanding.'

'I see.' Rachel wondered if she had ever felt so wretched. She couldn't imagine so, not even when her parents died. 'So—you want to call it off?'

Jake swore softly under his breath, and then began to walk slowly along the parade. Although her legs felt decidedly unsteady, she fell into step beside him, reminded of the first time they had walked together, and his anger on that occasion.

'Jake,' she probed despairingly. 'Jake, please! Don't do this.'

He stopped again to confront her, and her pulses raced at the look in his eyes. 'Rachel, you know as well as I do that what you're really looking for is a father figure—'

'*No!*'

'—someone to take the place of your parents.'

'No!' she cried again. 'That's not true. I loved my parents, of course I did, but when they died I didn't feel as I do now.'

'What do you mean?'

'Jake, if you leave me now, I—' She broke off, shaking back the tears. 'I love *you*! The man you are—*exactly* as you are! I don't want anyone else.'

'But—' Jake's hands balled into fists in his pockets. 'You saw what I was like yesterday. I'm still a wreck! You shouldn't waste your youth on someone like me.'

'For heaven's sake!' Rachel pressed her lips tightly together. 'What youth am I going to have if you walk out on me?'

Jake closed his eyes, and for an awful moment she thought he was ill until he opened them again to stare at her searchingly. 'I'm not worth it, you know,' he muttered roughly, and her heart palpitated madly.

'Just tell me if you want me,' she breathed, and for an answer he put his arm across her shoulders and pulled her close against him.

'You know I want you,' he groaned, pressing her head into the hollow of his neck. 'All right, on your head be it. But don't say I didn't warn you.'

'Oh, stop it!' Rachel looked up at him impatiently, trembling with reaction, and hardly capable of maintaining the controlled behaviour he expected of her. 'Come on.' She grasped his hand. 'Let's go down on the beach. I'm shaking so much people will think I've got pneumonia!'

'Then we'll go and buy a ring,' he said firmly, ignoring her instinctive recoil. 'Because I want to put my mark of possession upon you, that's all.'

of then we kiss and say a long.' He said clearly upon
log between have mood, 'No one. I want to put on
ment of trust, from my children, she said.

CHAPTER SEVEN

RACHEL SIPPED her champagne and endeavoured to behave as if she was used to gatherings of this kind. Certainly she fitted into her surroundings, and her white lace
dress could hold its own with the best that any Paris
couturier could provide. Her wide-brimmed hat had been
discarded a little while before, but the tumbled mass of
auburn-gold curls that framed her somewhat bemused
features needed no further adornment.

She could see Jake right at the other end of the room,
his dark head visible among a mass of lighter ones, cool
and immaculate, mingling as she was supposed to be
doing. In his charcoal grey morning suit, he looked very
much the sophisticated individual he was, and there was
a certain arrogance in the way he took his guest's good
wishes for granted.

For her part, Rachel knew the high spot of the day
had been their wedding at the tiny village church of St
Agnes. It had seemed as if everyone who lived in Hardy
Lonsdale had turned out for the celebration, and the
church was crammed before the service.

Jake had invited few guests to the actual ceremony,
but afterwards, here at his parents' home, their number
had been swelled by succeeding carloads of well-
wishers, all of whom seemed to have known Jake for a
number of years. And had known Denise too, Rachel
had decided tensely, although they were unerringly
charming to her.

Nevertheless, they were not her friends, not yet, at

least, and her eyes searched desperately for the faces of
Della, and Carl, and one or two of the other guests from
the hotel, her only contribution to this noisy gathering.
Never had Della's plump features looked so dearly familiar, and Rachel pushed her way between a group of
Mr Courtenay's horse-racing friends to where her erst-
while employer was holding court with Jake's mother,
his aunt, and two of his cousins. They were people Rachel had been introduced to before the ceremony, but
she couldn't remember any of their names now.

'Rachel!' Mrs Courtenay turned at her approach, and
smiled warmly. Since the marriage had become a definite possibility, she had done her utmost to make amends
for her earlier behaviour, and although Rachel still regarded her with a certain amount of caution, she had to
admit that Jake's mother had been very kind to her. It
was because of her that Rachel was now wearing this
model gown, purchased by Mrs Courtenay through her
connections with the London fashion houses, and in spite
of Rachel's protest that she had enough clothes, one or
two other items had found their way into her wardrobe.

'Such a beautiful dress,' sighed Mrs King admiringly,
as she joined them. 'You're a lucky girl, Rachel.'

'Yes.'

Rachel's husky affirmative was less than enthusiastic,
and Della gave her a curious look. 'Are you planning to
stay here until after Christmas?' she inquired. 'Aren't
you having a honeymoon?'

Rachel sighed. 'Jake still hasn't to overdo things,' she
explained, and his mother hastened to add that she and
Mr Courtenay were leaving that evening to spend a few
days with her sister in Dorchester.

'Naturally, we don't want to intrude,' she added
archly, 'although the west wing is quite apart from our

rooms at the other side of the house. Still, I always think a newly married couple need a little time alone together, don't you?'

'Stop embarrassing the girl, Sarah,' exclaimed her sister, earning her new niece's undying gratitude for her intervention. 'Jake and Rachel have all their lives ahead of them. There's time enough to be alone.'

'You're just like Charles, Lydia,' exclaimed Mrs Courtenay impatiently. 'You both behave as if you've never been young yourselves.'

Jake's Aunt Lydia merely gave a wry smile and turned to Rachel: 'Are you happy, my dear?' she asked. 'That's the important thing.'

Rachel managed a faint smile in return. 'Very happy,' she said, and the older women nodded.

Carl moved round to her as conversation became more general. 'I haven't been able to tell you before, but you look beautiful,' he murmured softly, his lips brushing her hair as he bent to speak into her ear. 'Courtenay's a lucky swine!'

Rachel expelled a trembling breath. 'You didn't always think so.'

Carl pulled a knowing face. 'I did, you know. Don't you recognise jealousy when you see it?'

'I shall miss you, Carl—all of you!' she added, in case he misunderstood. 'You're my last ties with the past. It's odd, but I never realised that until now.'

'You're not regretting it?' he exclaimed sharply, but she quickly shook her head.

'Oh, no. It was—inevitable, somehow. I knew that as soon, as—well, as soon as I saw Jake.'

'Love at first sight,' remarked Carl rather sceptically, but she shook her head.

'Not that, exactly. Just—a feeling. An awareness. I can't explain what it's like. I just know it's there.'

Carl expelled his breath heavily. 'Well, I hope he never disappoints you, that's all. His marriage to Denise was a disaster.'

'I know that.' Strangely the thought of Jake's first wife didn't trouble her so much now. 'But I'm going to make him happy.'

Carl compressed his lips, sensing the barrier she was deliberately erecting between them. He moved away as one of Jake's cousins came to offer her good wishes, and Rachel felt curiously sorry for him.

A hand at her elbow banished these thoughts, however, as Jake's quiet tones invaded her reverie: 'Do you want some more champagne?'

She glanced round at him at once, her heart quickening at the realisation that he was her husband now. 'I—no.' She gestured towards her still half-full glass. 'Is everything all right?'

'You tell me,' he answered gravely. 'I saw you with Yates. What was he saying to you?'

She gave a breathy little laugh. 'Are you jealous?'

'Yes.'

His reply was as unexpected as it was off-hand, spoken in a throw-away tone that in no way drew attention to the importance of its meaning. Rachel gazed up at him wideeyed, and her lips parted in confusion.

'Carl was just—admiring my dress,' she got out jerkily. 'Jake, you have no need to be jealous of him!'

His eyes moved meaningfully over the vee-necked bodice of her gown, lingering on the shadowy cleft between her breasts, just visible above the fine lace. 'Was that all he said?' he demanded, not acknowledging her protest, and she sighed.

'Yes. At least—well, he said you were a lucky swine, but that's a matter of opinion, isn't it?' she joked, and then getting no obvious response: 'How—much longer will this affair be going on?'

Jake's hand slid down her arm to her wrist, his fingers stroking her palm before interlacing themselves with hers. 'I thought I heard Denise's name mentioned,' he drawled quietly, his lips brushing close to her ear, as Carl's had done, but with infinitely more effect on Rachel. 'I hope you're not going to start lying to me this early in our relationship.'

Rachel turned to him aghast, but what she had been about to say was swallowed up by Mr Courtenay's booming voice, exclaiming loudly: 'Give someone else a chance, Jake! Can't you wait until you get her alone before you start monopolising the girl?'

Jake's father had obviously been imbibing too freely in the vintage champagne, and his face was unnaturally flushed and blotchy. Beads of perspiration stood out on his brow, and he occasionally mopped them away with a white handkerchief.

Mrs Courtenay, who had heard her husband's outburst, interposed herself between him and Rachel. 'You've had nothing to eat yet, Charles,' she said severely. 'Come along. I had Dora prepare some smoked salmon rolls especially for you.'

'I'm not hungry, Sarah!' protested Mr Courtenay irritably, and Jake released Rachel to take his father's arm.

'Come on,' he said tolerantly. 'You don't want to appear on the front page of the *Glastonbury Herald*, do you?'

His father blustered. 'The *Herald*? I thought you said there were to be no reporters here!'

'There aren't,' remarked Jake dryly, leading him

away. 'But you wouldn't know that for sure, would you?'

After they had gone, Mrs Courtenay shook her head in annoyance at her sister. 'Really!' she exclaimed. 'You'd think he would have more sense, at his age.'

'Oh, Sarah!' Lydia just laughed. 'He's enjoying himself. Leave him alone!'

Rachel tried to join in the general amusement, but her nerves were jumping after what Jake had said. She searched desperately for the sight of her husband coming back again, but it was Della who drew her to one side and said: 'What's the matter? You look—pale.'

'I'm all right.' The last thing Rachel needed right now was advice from Della. 'It's warm in here, isn't it?'

Della gave her a narrow look. 'You do know what you're letting yourself in for, don't you?' she murmured, in an undertone. 'Oh, yes, I suppose you must do. Young people these days—they don't bother waiting for the wedding to give them licence to go to bed together.'

Rachel was stung by her words. 'If you're implying that Jake and I have already been to bed together, then you couldn't be more wrong!' she declared hotly.

'No?' Della was obviously surprised. 'I'd never have taken Jake for an ascetic!'

Rachel bent her head. 'Please don't spoil things, Della.'

'I'm not trying to.' For once Della seemed sincere. 'But—well, whether you like it or not, I am the nearest thing to a mother you're likely to find today, and perhaps we should—talk about things.'

'I know the facts of life, Della.'

'I'm sure you do.' Della glanced round casually to make sure their conversation was not being overheard, and then went on: 'But between theories and their practical counterparts there's an enormous gulf.'

'Della, please—'

'No. Listen to me: I know what I'm talking about. I've been married, remember. I know what it's like.'

Rachel sighed, and looked round hopefully for Jake; but he and his father were standing by the buffet tables, apparently deep in conversation, and short of walking off and leaving her, she was obliged to listen to what the older woman had to say.

'Of course,' Della mused, 'marrying an older man makes it a little better for you. I mean, Jake has had experience, hasn't he? But—be warned. It's not the romantic event you imagine it to be.'

'Has that been your experience, Mrs Faulkner-Stewart?'

Unobserved, Jake had returned, and was now standing behind Rachel, listening to their conversation with a, distinct lack of self-consciousness. But Della's plump face turned crimson.

'Why, Mr Courtenay,' she exclaimed, pressing a hand to her breast. 'I didn't see you there.' She cleared her throat. 'I—er—I was just trying to explain to Rachel that—that women don't necessarily feel about these things as a man does.'

'What things?' Jake was evidently enjoying himself, and the hand he slid around Rachel's waist, drawing her back against him, was definitely possessive.

Della could not have looked more embarrassed. 'I know you're only teasing me, Mr Courtenay,' she exclaimed, striving to sound coquettish. 'Tell me, what does it feel like being married again?'

'Infinitely better than before,' responded Jake lightly, dropping a casual caress on the side of his wife's neck.

'But now, if you'll excuse us, there's someone I want Rachel to meet.'

Away from Della's knowing eyes, Rachel turned to him anxiously. 'Jake! About—about before—about Denise—'

'Not now, Rachel,' he told her smoothly. 'There really is someone I want to introduce you to. My consultant— Maxwell Francis.'

Maxwell Francis was a man in his late forties, Rachel surmised. Tall, heavier built than his patient, with piercing blue eyes and a bristling beard and moustache, he looked more like an artist than a doctor. But his manner was gentle, and she guessed he inspired confidence in the people he treated.

'I never expected Jake to arrive back from Devon with a wife, Mrs Courtenay,' he commented smilingly, giving her an unknowing thrill at his casual use of her new designation. 'But, having met you, I can quite see why he was bowled over.'

'You don't think Rachel's kind of stimulation is a bad thing for me, then?' suggested Jake ironically, and the older man laughed.

'My dear fellow, I've been telling you for years that you spend far too much time in that office of yours. Perhaps now you'll feel more inclined to go home nights.'

Jake gave his wife a studied look. 'You might be right, Max,' he acknowledged mockingly, and Rachel felt her nails digging into her palms.

It was all right for Jake to torment her, but not, apparently, for her to do the same to him. On impulse, she linked both her arms with one of his, and deliberately pressing herself against him said: 'You will come home nights, won't you, darling?' in decidedly provocative tones.

His reaction was to gently, but firmly, disengage his arm from hers, and with heated cheeks, Rachel turned to the consultant.

'Are you married, doctor?' she asked tautly.

'Indeed I am.'

Rachel glanced round. 'Is your wife here with you?'

'I'm afraid not.' Then, in answer to her unspoken question, he added: 'My wife is in a nursing home at present, recovering from the birth of our third daughter just a week ago.'

'Oh!' Rachel gulped, 'So you have three daughters.'

'And a son,' agreed Maxwell Francis, nodding. 'He's the eldest, fortunately, or I've no doubt his life wouldn't be worth living with three sisters!'

Rachel relaxed a little. 'Please—give my best wishes to your wife and tell her I hope to meet her in person one day.'

'I'll certainly do that,' he said, with evident pleasure. 'You and Jake will have to come and visit us when you get back to London, We live just outside, actually, but Jake knows the way.'

'I'd like that.'

'So long as you don't mind a gang of children and a mad dog crawling all over you, you'll enjoy it,' put in Jake humorously, and Maxwell laughed again.

'Yes, that's the way of it,' he admitted.

'I shan't mind at all,' Rachel asserted. 'I like children.'

'Good,' Maxwell grinned. 'Then the next time I see you, I shall expect to hear there's a little Courtenay on the way.'

Rachel was taken aback by his frankness, but again

Jake came to the rescue. 'Not quite yet, Max,' he assured him firmly. 'I want my wife to myself for a while.'

A couple whom Rachel recognised as being business associates of Jake's came to join them just then, and conversation became less personal. John Masterson, as the man was called, was able to satisfy some of Jake's queries about his business affairs and while the two men were talking together, Mrs Masterson asked her how soon they expected to get back to London.

'Not until the New Year,' inserted Maxwell Francis, with some definition. 'Jake knows how I feel about it, and I don't approve of him talking shop at his own wedding reception.'

Hearing the consultant's final words, Jake broke off what he was saying to Masterson. 'All right, Max,' he said resignedly. 'I guess you're right. It isn't fair to Rachel, is it?'

Rachel caught his eyes upon her, and for once returned his stare without flinching. 'No, it isn't,' she said clearly, and they both knew she was not only referring to his conversation with Masterson.

Rachel's head was aching by the time the last carload of guests disappeared down the drive, and Mr and Mrs Courtenay prepared to leave. It had been arranged that Dora Pendlebury should spend the night at a friend's house in the village, and Sheila had already left for a short holiday in London. Rachel had been glad she was not going to have to face the housekeeper's daughter on her wedding day, although Jake's mother had expressed some regret that she should not be there. However, that was all in the past now, and Rachel's features felt stiff and cold as she stood beside Jake waving his parents off. Everything she had been told, all the wild stories she had heard at school and since, crowded into her tired head, and she trembled when she considered that whatever happened now, she was on her own.

When Mr Courtenay's Mercedes had disappeared, driven incidentally by Mrs Courtenay, Rachel turned at Jake's suggestion, and preceded him back into the house. It had been an unusually bright day for December, but it was over now, and darkness pressed closely around the old walls of the priory. A gusty wind occasionally rattled the window frames, and the leaping flames of the fire were a welcome sight.

Jake closed the heavy door and locked it, and then walked lazily across to the fire, kicking a log further into its glowing heart with one suede-booted foot. Now that they were alone, he took off his immaculate morning coat, and tugged his tie free of the collar of his shirt. His skin looked particularly dark against the pristine whiteness of the shirt, the gold chain around his neck visible as he unfastened the top two buttons.

Rachel stepped delicately across the floor towards him, and he studied her appearance through heavy-lidded eyes.

'Well?' he said evenly. 'That's that. The party's over.'

'Is it?' Rachel drew a deep breath. 'I thought everything went very well, didn't you?'

'Very well,' he conceded dryly. 'You carried it off beautifully. Everyone thinks I'm a very fortunate man.'

'Do you think that, too?' she ventured daringly, but he moved away towards the stairs, mounting them two at a time to reach the landing.

He stood looking down at her for a moment, and then he said abruptly: 'I need a shower,' and turned towards his rooms in the west wing.

Rachel waited a few minutes to see if he would come back, but when he didn't, she too mounted the stairs, standing uncertainly on the landing, wondering whether she was expected to find her own way to his apartments.

On impulse, she walked into the drawing room again, empty now that the caterers had cleared away the remains of the buffet, but still full of the scent of Havana tobacco; and from there into the small parlour where Dora had laid an intimate supper for two. How the housekeeper must have disliked doing this, Rachel thought with perception, recalling Dora's animosity towards herself. But if Jake had wanted to marry Sheila, he could have done so years ago, and they shouldn't blame her because he did not find the older girl attractive.

The table looked quite romantic. The napkins were red, and matched the centrepiece of glowing poinsettia, that spread its scarlet leaves in a bowl of dark green fern. There were fragile stemmed glasses, and glittering silverware, and two scented candles to light for illumination. Another bottle of champagne nestled in a bucket of crushed ice beside the table, and Rachel touched its frosted neck with hands that were not quite steady.

'Are you hungry?'

Jake's rubber soles made little sound on the soft carpets, and she started involuntarily, a hand going defensively to her throat. As she turned to look at him, she saw he had changed his clothes, but the close-fitting corded pants and maroon velvet jerkin were as attractive as his morning clothes had been.

'I—I was just admiring the table,' she told him, lifting her shoulders in a nervous little gesture. 'Mrs Pendlebury deserves to be complimented.'

'Dora!' Jake corrected her flatly. 'Her name is Dora. No one calls her Mrs Pendlebury.'

'She might prefer me to,' persisted Rachel. 'I mean, I hardly know the woman.'

'That can be remedied,' retorted Jake levelly. 'Now, do you want to eat first, or change?'

Rachel looked down at her dress. 'Change, I think,' she decided, trying to sound casual. 'I—well, I didn't know where I—*we* were going to sleep.'

'Come along, then. I'll show you.'

Jake escorted her into the west wing once more, passing the door which she knew led to the bedroom he used to use, and pausing outside double doors at the end of the corridor.

The room they entered was furnished as a sitting room, of medium size, with a comfortable high-backed sofa, and matching easy chairs, in a soft grape-coloured velour. But adjoining it was the bedroom, and Rachel hovered on the threshold, half dismayed by its size and opulence. The bed dominated the room, an enormous four-poster, with hanging curtains of beige-coloured silk, and a matching bedspread, whose tassels trailed on to the off-white carpet. It was the kind of room which hitherto she had only seen in the movies, and she simply could not imagine herself sleeping here.

'Do you like it?'

Jake's voice was vaguely sardonic, and she turned to look at him warily. 'I—it's beautiful,' she said politely, and he pulled a wry face.

'This is my mother's idea of a honeymoon suite,' he remarked mockingly. 'The bathroom's through there, and you'll see that she's had all your belongings transferred to the wardrobes here.'

Rachel licked her dry lips. 'I—I see.'

'I'll leave you to change,' he continued, straightening

from the indolent slouch he had adopted, and a few moments later the outer doors closed behind him.

The bathroom was just as luxurious, with gold-plated taps, and a creamy-yellow sunken tub. Wall mirrors were embarrassing, frankly reflecting her slender body from all angles, and she was glad when the steam misted them over and hid her blushes.

Back in the bedroom again, Rachel opened the doors of a tall wardrobe and surveyed the contents hanging there. Her clothes, brought from the hotel, fitted into less than half its width, but the new garments Mrs Courtenay had bought her helped to fill the empty space. Among them was a filmy green chiffon, and it was this that Rachel took out and laid reverently on the bed.

Her make-up took little time, although she gave some attention to her eyes, stroking mascara on to her lashes, and a luminous green shadow to her lids. Then she slipped the filmy gown over her head and allowed its sinuous folds to settle lovingly about the slender curves of her body. Surveying her reflection in the long mirrors of the wardrobe, she had to admit that she had never worn anything that gave her such a sensuous appeal.

Trembling a little, she turned from the mirror and ran unsteady fingers over her hair. She was ready, and in spite of the confidence the gown had given her, she was still nervous. The things Della had said kept coming back to torment her, and Jake's own attitude of detachment did not help matters.

Leaving the bedroom, she crossed the lounge and emerged into the corridor. Although the whole of the building was centrally heated, the corridor felt cooler as the wind outside probed every crack in the stonework, sending ice-cold fingers of chill to penetrate the gauzy folds of her gown. It quickened her step towards the lighted doorway of the drawing room, and she was glad to step inside and close the doors behind her.

Jake must have heard her coming, for he came out of the parlour to meet her. She waited breathlessly for his reaction to her appearance, and felt a sense of anti-climax when his eyes moved over her and slid away as he said: 'Would you like some champagne, or shall we eat first?'

Rachel shrugged her slim shoulders. 'Whichever you want to do,' she said breathily. 'Jake—'

'We'll have some champagne,' he cut in on her, and she was forced to follow him into the parlour. The candles Dora had provided had been lighted, but they were supplemented by the light from the branched chandelier suspended above the table, and Rachel wondered whether Jake's earlier mood was responsible for this lack of intimacy.

While he uncorked the bottle, she seated herself at the table, resting her elbows on the white napery, cupping her chin in her hands. Her nervousness was giving way to other emotions, and she wished she knew how to break down the barrier he was deliberately building between them. She attracted him, who could doubt that? But could she overcome whatever it was that was causing that unsmiling reserve?

Using what little guile she possessed, she tipped her head on one side and said: 'You haven't noticed my dress.'

Jake gripped the champagne bottle between his thighs as he bent to draw the cork. 'I noticed,' he responded flatly, and she felt her nails digging into her palms.

Refusing to be deterred, she added: 'Do you like it?' and was somewhat chastened by the look he directed towards her.

The cork came out with a bang, and foaming liquid overran the sides of the bottle. 'Have some champagne,' Jake advised, filling her glass, and she permitted herself a half-suppressed sigh of frustration before tasting the wine.

It was delicious, and she swallowed what was in her glass quite quickly in an effort to give herself more confidence. Jake, who had taken his seat, leant across to refill her glass, and it crossed her mind that if she was not careful, she would overdo it. She wasn't used to alcohol in any form, and she had eaten little enough today to absorb an abundance of fluid.

The meal was a simple one: a cold consommé was followed by sliced meats with salad, and the gateau to finish was oozing with cream. Throughout the meal, Rachel drank as little as possible, although it was difficult to get anything down her parched throat without liquid. However, the soup went down quite freely, and the gateau displaced her discomfort at not doing justice to the salad.

Jake spoke little as they ate, and Rachel's efforts to introduce a lighter note into the proceedings all went unacknowledged. But at last it was over, and Jake brought to the table the jug of coffee which had been keeping hot over a small burner.

'A liqueur, I think, would not come amiss,' he remarked, uncorking another bottle, but Rachel looked up at him apologetically.

'Not for me, thank you,' she refused, forcing a smile to her lips. 'Are you trying to get me drunk?'

Jake's eyes narrowed. 'That would be a futile exercise, wouldn't it?' he challenged, and she was forced to look away.

'I just thought—'

'I'd like you to try this liqueur,' he persisted. 'Won't you? For me?'

It was the nearest he had got to saying anything personal to her all evening, and Rachel drew a trembling breath. 'Well—all right,' she conceded unwillingly. 'But—just a little.'

'Of course.'

The glasses they used were thimble-size, and Rachel relaxed. No one could get drunk on so little alcohol. But its fiery quality burned her throat, and the first mouthful had her coughing ignominiously.

'What is it?' she exclaimed huskily.

Jake lifted his glass and studied its contents. 'Just a liquorice root liqueur,' he assured her evenly. 'Don't you think it's rather a beautiful colour?'

Rachel looked at the lucid green liquid in her glass. 'Liquorice?' she echoed faintly. 'I thought liquorice was black.'

'It is.' Jake regarded her half mockingly. 'Drink it up. It's good for you.'

Rachel's head felt strange. There was an awful swimming sensation if she moved it too quickly, and her eyes felt heavy as lead. Oh, God, she thought impatiently, she must have had too much to drink in spite of her precautions.

'Shall we adjourn to the drawing room?' Jake inquired, still watching her, and she nodded her head with deliberate care and got to her feet.

He thought she was drunk, she decided angrily. Well, she would show him that she was not. She had read somewhere that it was only a matter of time before the effects of alcohol wore off. If she could just sit down quietly for a while, she would soon feel normal again.

She turned from the table, loath to leave the security

of her chair. Perhaps she should have refused to go into the drawing room. Maybe if she stayed at the table and tried to eat a little more of the meat that still nestled in its bed of celery and diced melon. But the thought of food right now was nauseating, and the idea of being sick and ruining her beautiful gown didn't bear thinking about.

Jake was standing a little way away from her, the glass he held casually between his long fingers still quite full. Of course, he had told her, he should not imbibe too freely, and the way he stood there, feet apart, regarding her with almost inimical detachment, was indicative of his own sobriety. And she resented it…

The door leading into the drawing room wavered before her eyes and she steeled herself for the seemingly endless stretch of floor that divided her from remembered couches where she might lay her aching head. Her wedding day, she thought with some self-pity! And she had almost ruined it. Or was that Jake? She tried to think coherently. What was it he had said earlier, before that wall of indifference had descended between them?

'Do you need some help?'

Jake's cool voice seemed to come from a great distance, and she was shocked to find him standing right beside her.

'No,' she declared vehemently. 'I'm all right. I can manage.'

'Are you sure?'

Was that concern in his tones? Did he actually reveal a little anxiety now? Rachel blinked and stared at him defensively. 'I've told you. I'm all right. That—that liqueur—it—I didn't like it.'

'I'm sorry.'

He was polite, but the dryness was back in his voice

and she wished she could think of some politely sarcastic retort which would wipe that cool detachment from his face.

She couldn't. It was no use. Her brain was muzzy along with the rest of her faculties, and clenching her fists, she started across the floor. But the floor was behaving in a most unusual way, too, dipping and weaving so that the pattern on the carpet swam into a haze of green and gold that made her eyes ache with weariness. Oh, to close her eyes, she thought longingly, and wondered at the hard hands that reached for her before unconsciousness claimed her...

CHAPTER EIGHT

JAKE'S LONDON APARTMENT was the penthouse suite of
a block in a square near Hyde Park. In fact, it was possible to see the whole of the metropolitan area from its
windows, and Rachel had not been immune from the
sense of space the view generated.

The apartment itself was no surprise to her after the
magnificence of the Priory, although the overall effect
was less opulent and more modern. A split-level lounge
and dining area was an architectural attraction, and the
kitchen was all steel and gleaming formica. There were
four bedrooms, each with its own bathroom, and a study
where Jake told her he was used to spending his leisure
hours. Every amenity for ease and efficiency of operation had been installed, and the place was run very com-
petently by a married couple who themselves had a flat
in the basement.

The Madigans, as they were called, treated Rachel
with respect, and with none of the hostility of Dora Pendlebury. She was relieved about this, even though their
attitude left no room for familiarity either. They seemed
to keep themselves very much to themselves, and she
found herself wondering whether that was why Jake had
felt so little attraction to his home in the past. But the
whole aspect of her life had changed to such an extent
that she had little enthusiasm in those early days to pon-
der other people's relationships. Besides, what experience had she in such matters? She had thought she knew
Jake, but she was beginning to wonder.

She had awakened on the morning after her wedding to find herself alone in the enormous wastes of cream silk sheets, with the imprint of only her head on the pillow denoting the solitary night she had spent. That her clothes had been removed and that she was naked in the bed had given her a momentary thrill of apprehension, but she had not needed any self-examination to know that Jake had not violated her unresisting lack of consciousness.

Bathed and dressed, she had gone in search of her husband, only to discover he was not in the house, and only Dora was about, clearing their dishes from the night before, and tidying the living rooms. She had given the girl a frosty greeting, and although she offered breakfast Rachel had refused everything but coffee.

When Jake eventually came in from the stables, he had found his new wife curled up on a sofa in the drawing room feeling very much alone and abandoned. And his first words had not been reassuring to her: 'Did you sleep well?'

At this, Rachel had swung her legs to the floor and got to her feet. She had been eager not to let the night's events determine their future relationship.

'I'm afraid I must have passed out,' she said apologetically. 'I'm sorry.'

'You were tired,' he corrected her, moving to the hearth where Dora had re-lit the fire.

In close-fitting denim pants and a grey knitted shirt he was disruptively attractive, and she wanted to go to him and put her arms about him and show him how much she loved him. Two days before she would not have hesitated, but somehow something had changed, and now she found herself wondering what he would have done if she had followed her instincts.

'Jake,' she had said instead, unconsciously appealing. 'Jake…can we talk?'

'Are we not?' he countered, and she felt the same sense of defeat she had felt the night before. But she would not let him get away with it.

'Jake…since yesterday afternoon—'

'After the wedding?'

'Yes.' She paused. 'Jake, has something happened? Is something wrong? Why are you treating me this way?'

Her outburst at least had the effect of bringing a little more colour to his unnaturally sallow cheeks. But his eyes remained bleak as he surveyed her. 'I tried to tell you how it would be,' he spoke at last, slowly. 'You knew it wasn't going to be easy, but believe me, it is the only way.'

'The only way?' Rachel shook her head helplessly. She felt as if she was confronted by some enormously complicated puzzle, and as yet she had no clue to its solution. 'The only way to—*what*?'

Jake sighed now, his patience thinning. 'Rachel, I'm talking about you—and me! I told you, we need time to get to know one another—'

'And you think we will? Treating one another like strangers?' she protested.

Jake made a frustrated gesture. 'I explained—I married you to get you away from Della Faulkner-Stewart. There was no other way. She would never have allowed you to leave her and come with me without creating the kind of scandal I most wanted to avoid, but that doesn't mean the situation is any easier.'

She felt a sense of coldness invading her stomach. 'What are you trying to say?'

'What I've said all along, Rachel. We're married— but that need only be a formality.'

'A formality!' Her agitation was visible. 'Jake, I love you!'

'So you say.' His tone was dry.

'I mean it.' She spread her hands. 'Jake, let me show you—'

'No.' Automatically, he stepped back from her. 'Rachel, can't you accept that for the next few months things have got to remain as they are? Surely that's not so impossible? Give our relationship time to develop—in all directions. I must be sure that what you—*think* you feel for me is more than just infatuation.'

Rachel tugged painful fingers through her hair. She could hardly take this in. She hardly wanted to take it in. Wanting to hurt him as he was hurting her, she exclaimed: 'And what if it is? Infatuation, I mean. What then?'

'The marriage can be annulled, as I've said.'

'You're so cold-blooded,' she cried unable to sustain an air of detachment. 'I thought you loved me!'

'I do care about you, Rachel,' he declared stiffly, and then meeting her tormented gaze, he turned away to kick savagely at the logs in the grate. 'I do,' he repeated harshly. 'But there is no middle way, Rachel. That's why we have to try and make one. If I were to go on as before, there would be no turning back. Knowing you were my wife, do you think I could let you go?'

'I don't want you to let me go,' she breathed, welcoming the glimmer of emotion that overran his words, but when he turned to her again, he had himself in control once more.

'A few weeks,' he said firmly. 'If we're going to spend the rest of our lives together, a few weeks won't make that much difference.'

Rachel's shoulders sagged. 'So you really were trying to get me drunk last night.'

Jake sighed. 'You were overwrought, Rachel. I had to do something. Could you think of a better way?'

Rachel shook her head helplessly. 'A deliberate plan,' she said bitterly. 'And I thought I'd let you down.'

Jake stifled an oath. 'We have so much to learn about one another—'

'I'm beginning to believe it.'

'—but if there's to be no trust between us...'

Rachel drew a deep breath. 'So what you're really saying is that we should live as—individuals—for the next few weeks.'

'Friends, I hope.'

'Friends?' She turned away, feeling completely shattered. 'And—and when your parents come back? What then? Won't they think it strange that you—that we don't share the same bedroom?'

'Not necessarily. I've been ill, as my mother is so fond of pointing out. If it becomes general knowledge, I shall tell her that as I don't rest very easily, I sleep alone to avoid disturbing you.'

'You have it all worked out, don't you?' she exclaimed tremulously, sick with the realisation that he was adamant in what he said. It was humiliating to know he could dismiss the intimacies of their marriage so carelessly, while she ached with longings which until recently she had not known she possessed. Was there nothing she could say to change his mind?

Expelling an unsteady breath, she began: 'Jake—yesterday; when—when Carl was talking to me, you asked whether—whether we had discussed Denise...'

'Well?'

Rachel hesitated. His eyes were so cold. She shivered.

'I—well, all he said was that—that your marriage to her was unhappy. You said you were jealous. That—that's not why—'

'No!' He spoke vehemently, and her voice tailed away. He looked at her silently for a few moments, and then he added: 'I have to repeat, you knew my feelings about this marriage before the wedding, but just because I'm prepared to give you time to adapt before taking that irretrievable step it does not mean I don't have all the normal feelings of any husband confronted by his wife's attraction for another man.'

'I'm not attracted to Carl!' Rachel denied hotly, and Jake raised one dark eyebrow.

'We shall see, shan't we?' he remarked wryly, and she wrapped her arms protectively about herself.

'You really mean to go through with this, don't you?' she challenged him painfully, but the question was a perfunctory one. She already knew the answer.

That was all four weeks ago now, and in those four weeks Rachel had learned one thing at least—the art of hiding her feelings. With the return of Jake's parents, and Sheila Pendlebury's constant presence about the Priory, she had soon cultivated a defensive shell within which she could nurse her vulnerable emotions without fear of observation.

To the Courtenays, she endeavoured to appear happy and relaxed, although it was often an effort, particularly at mealtimes. Food no longer had any real appeal for her, and she ate for the sole purpose of avoiding painful comment. Jake noticed, of course, and remarked upon her fining features in private, but with him she was scarcely civil anyway, and in his father's house there was little he could do.

Jake spent a lot of his time at the stables, but although

Rachel was attracted to the horses, she maintained an indifference in an effort to gain some reaction from him. She didn't have a lot of experience with men, however, and her unsophisticated attempts to arouse his antagonism and through it his emotions bore little fruit.

On one occasion, bored by her own company and having refused Mrs Courtenay's invitation to join her on a shopping expedition and knowing Jake was working with the horses, she had put on her coat and left the house. It was a cold, frosty afternoon, only a few days before Christmas, and her intention was to ask Jake if he would drive her into Glastonbury. She had some foolish idea of buying him a present with a slice of the unused allowance he was paying her, and maybe reaching him in that way. But before she had even reached the stables, she had heard Sheila's husky laughter and guessed that her husband was not alone. The temptation to turn back there and then was strong, but anger had driven her forward and in through the open stable door.

As she had expected, Sheila was there, her tall slim figure attractively clad in matching pants and jacket of lovat tweed, a red scarf slotted at the open neck complementing the darkness of her hair. She was leaning over the stall where Jake was grooming one of the horses, helping him up from a squatting position, and he, too, looked easy and relaxed. That they were both surprised to see Rachel was obvious, and Rachel did not stop to think before rushing into reckless accusation.

'Oh, I'm sorry,' she exclaimed with heavy sarcasm, 'am I intruding? I thought you were busy, Jake, but obviously that only applies so far as I'm concerned!'

'Rachel!'

Jake straightened, his dark face flushed with anger, but she went on as if she had not heard him: 'Perhaps I should have knocked before entering, or used the intercom system to let you know I was coming! I was going to ask you to take me into Glastonbury, but of course what you're doing here is far more important!'

And with these childish words, born out of the desire to show him she was not afraid to speak her mind, she turned and marched out of the stables again, ignoring his furious utterance of her name.

But her new-found courage would not permit her to walk back to the house. Her steps gradually quickened until she was practically running, and she had turned the corner of the priory before Jake emerged and was therefore unaware that he was following her.

She let herself into the hall with a feeling of dismay unsettling the uncertain nerves in the pit of her stomach. Common sense was asserting itself again, and the realisation of what she had said brought a wave of hot colour to her cheeks. Jake would be so angry, and as for Sheila... She caught her lower lip between her teeth. So far she and the older girl had maintained a kind of cautious neutrality, but she had destroyed that now.

She had reached the stairs when the heavy door opened behind her, and glancing round anxiously she saw her husband's grim figure. He had pulled on a leather jerkin over the heavy sweater and jeans he had been wearing to work in, and the dark colours accentuated his brooding countenance.

Unable to withstand his denigrating appraisal, she turned swiftly and ran up the stairs, the hammering of her heart in her ears drowning any sounds of his pursuit. She reached her door only seconds before he did, and she was trembling violently when he thrust her ahead of him into the room. The door slammed heavily behind them, and it was only by a great effort of will-power that she stopped herself from making an undignified dash for the safety of the bathroom and its securing bolt.

Jake stared at her angrily for several seconds, and then he said savagely: 'Don't you ever do that to me again!'

Rachel separated her chattering teeth with her tongue. 'And—and if I choose to do so?' she returned jerkily. 'How will you stop me? I don't understand why—why you didn't marry her! At least with her you wouldn't need time to get to know one another. You seem—you seem to know one another very well as—as it is!'

Jake regarded her grimly for a few more terrifying moments, and then with a violent ejaculation he reached for her, jerking her into his arms with a roughness that made her lose her balance and fall helplessly against him. His lips imprisoned her startled mouth, until her lips parted wilfully, allowing him full possession of the moist sweetness within. One hand was beneath her hair at her nape, while the other slid the length of her spine, moulding her body against his with increasing intimacy.

'All right,' he muttered, releasing her lips to turn his mouth against the soft curve of her throat, 'if you persist in baiting me...'

His mouth covered hers again, but this time his hand went behind her legs, swinging her feet off the ground so that he could carry her into the bedroom and put her down on the silken bedspread. Uncaring of his boots, or that he had come straight from the stables, he flung himself beside her, and the weight of his body was an intoxicating accompaniment to the stirring urgency of her senses.

Whether he would have gone the whole way and taken her in anger, she was never to know. No sooner had his fingers unfastened the buttons of her shirt exposing the rose-tipped fullness of her breasts to his caressing touch, than someone started knocking at the outer door of the suite and Dora's voice could be heard calling that Jake was wanted on the telephone.

There was a moment when she thought he was going to ignore the housekeeper's summons, when his tongue stroked the hardening nipples, and her heart leapt with a mixture of fear and excited anticipation. But then, with a groan, he dragged himself away from her to stand beside the bed looking down at her with impassioned eyes.

'Jake...' she breathed, raising herself on her elbows, deliberately leaving the buttons of her shirt unloosened, knowing that he was not indifferent to the sensuous softness of her flesh. But he turned abruptly away and when next he spoke his voice was harsh:

'Consider yourself reprieved,' he said. 'Or perhaps the reprieve is mine, hmm? I'm not usually so susceptible to provocation!'

And he had gone, leaving her to pull herself together, both physically and mentally, unable to deny the surge of resentment she felt towards Dora, although the housekeeper was in no way responsible for the ill-timed significance of the phone call. *Or was she?* In her distraught state, Rachel was prepared to believe that Sheila might well have had something to do with that inappropriate interruption.

Christmas had not been an easy festival. Rachel had had cards from several of the people at the hotel, including Della, but it was Carl's greeting which increased the antipathy between herself and Jake. It was a simple enough message, written on a bright, if overly large, card, but the situation between herself and her husband was such that any small disagreement could escalate out of all proportion. The position was aggravated by Sheila commenting upon the size of the card and making coy insinuations about Rachel having an admirer. Of course, Rachel understood Sheila's motivations; she was less certain of Jake's.

The outcome was that the card disappeared altogether on Christmas Eve, and although that event in itself was not important, Rachel was convinced that Jake had destroyed it, and made a big thing of it at the dinner table. Half way through an embarrassing altercation with Jake, Dora interrupted them to say that *she* had accidentally knocked the card off the mantelpiece and into the fire, and had hoped that no one would notice one among so many.

It was exactly the kind of humiliation needed to crack Rachel's failing efforts at composure, and she had left the table at once, her handkerchief pressed tightly to her lips. She had half expected Jake to follow her—half expected his parents might suggest he should do so—but she had been mistaken. She had spent a lonely evening in her room and an even lonelier night...

Christmas Day had proved to be slightly less fraught. Dora had been given the day off, Mrs Courtenay assuring her that she and Rachel could handle the already-prepared turkey, and when gifts were exchanged at the breakfast table, Rachel had been warmed by Jake's parents' presentation of a silver cross and chain. They told her it had been given to Jake when he was christened by his grandmother, Mr Courtenay's mother, and had been in the Courtenay family for generations. Her own gifts to them were much less valuable—a lace shawl for Mrs Courtenay, and a new pipe for Jake's father, but they seemed delighted.

She had not expected a gift from Jake, particularly not in the circumstances, but she had counted without his desire to maintain the illusion of their marriage for his parents' sake. His gift to her was a matching set of earrings and necklace, delicately cut sapphires and rubies adorning slender gold chains, that swung from her ears when she moved her head, or rested with fragile fire against her warm skin. She didn't know what to say when she lifted the lid of the jeweller's box, or how to thank him with his parents watching her every move.

'They're beautiful!' she murmured inadequately, meeting his gaze with uncertain eyes, only too aware of the gulf that was stretching between them. 'Thank you.'

Jake inclined his head casually, apparently intent on examining the diamond-studded cufflinks his mother had given him, but Mr Courtenay was not to be deprived of a more demonstrative approach.

'Give him a kiss, girl!' he exclaimed jovially, puffing away at his new pipe, and Rachel felt obliged to get up out of her chair and approach her husband. She half expected him to repulse her, and was therefore shocked when Jake's hand went behind her head as she bent to him, guiding her mouth to his and sharing with her a kiss that was as sensual as it was unexpected. Rachel's eyes were puzzled when she reluctantly lifted her head, but she gained no further knowledge from the guarded depths of his.

During the short wintry afternoon that followed the traditional Christmas dinner, they all relaxed around the fire in the drawing room, toasting chestnuts and sharing the kind of family intimacy Rachel had never really known with her parents. Sitting with Jake on one of the huge sofas, she knew that all she needed to make her world complete was for Jake to want her as much as she wanted him, to tell her he loved her—something he had never done, she realised with a pang...

But maybe the New Year would bring her the hap-

piness she sought, she thought with an attempt at opti-
mism. Maybe now that they were living at Jake's London apartment, he would realise that her feelings for him
were no fleeting infatuation.

They had driven up to London ten days after Christmas, and Rachel had made her first acquaintance with
her new home. She would have preferred them to have
a house, with a garden, but she realised that Jake needed
to be central for business purposes, and after a week in
London she began to appreciate just how demanding
Jake's work could be. She wasn't at all sure that Maxwell Francis would approve of the way Jake had immediately taken up the strains of his previous existence,
although she had to admit he wasn't given a lot of choice
in the matter. Once the news got around that he was
back, the phone never seemed to stop ringing, and although Mrs Madigan invariably answered it, Rachel
grew to hate the sound of the telephone bell.

The changes in her life from that which she had led
at the Priory were not so different. Her surroundings
were different, of course, but she had grown accustomed
to seeing little of Jake during the day, and her main
difficulty was in finding ways to fill her time. It wasn't
enough for Jake to say that she had the use of a car or
an allowance that might comfortably have fed a family
of four. She wanted to be part of his life, not just an
onlooker on the sidelines. How else were they to get to
know one another?

Jake usually managed to get home in time to shower
and change for dinner at around seven-thirty. This was
the high spot of Rachel's day, although invariably after
the meal was over he took himself off to his study for
a couple of hours, only emerging when she was thinking
of going to bed. She guessed he was trying to show her

how difficult it was being the wife of a man like him, but if he was prepared to spend his nights with her, she would suffer the days gladly.

Now. Rachel looked at her watch. It was almost seven, and she had been sitting staring unseeingly at her reflection in her vanity unit for the past half hour. Jake should have been home by now, but she had not heard him come in, and as his bedroom was adjacent to hers, she could usually detect some sounds when he was changing or taking his shower. She herself had showered some time ago, and lying on the bed was another of the dresses Mrs Courtenay had chosen, a primrose-yellow silk jersey, with a high roll collar and hip-flaring skirt. To think, she thought wryly, only a couple of months ago she had seen Della in this position, and now... She had never envied the older woman, but although she would not change her life now, she envied the girl she used to be.

A door slammed somewhere, and she started nervously. Jake must be home. She licked her dry lips and picked up her mascara brush to finish darkening the golden tips of her lashes. It wouldn't take her more than a minute to put on her dress and Jake would need at least half an hour to bathe and change. Her pulses quickened as they always did when she thought of him, and she felt an impatience with herself. She was a married woman now, not a schoolgirl on her first date. She must learn to control her foolish emotions.

There was a sudden knock at her door, and the mascara brush smudged her cheek. 'Damn!' she mouthed silently, and then called: 'Who is it?'

'Me,' came the laconic reply, and she dropped the brush nervelessly on to the tray. 'Can I come in?'

Rachel got to her feet, wrapping her silk robe closer about her slender form. It was the first time Jake had come to her door in the four weeks of their marriage, and while her thundering heart told her one thing, cold common sense warned her not to jump to conclusions.

'Yes,' she said now. 'Come—come in!'

The door opened and Jake entered, still wearing his dark city clothes. He looked tired, she thought anxiously, but he wouldn't welcome her saying that, and instead she concentrated on the dark, sallow-skinned features and lean muscled body she ached to touch.

His gaze moved over her swiftly, then pushing back his hair with a weary hand, he said: 'We've been invited out this evening. Do you mind?'

Rachel's heart-rate subsided. 'Out?' she echoed faintly. 'Er—out where?'

Jake sighed. 'It's a party, actually. Being given by Jon and Petra Forrest, some—friends of mine. He's a business acquaintance actually, but I've known the pair of them for years. I thought it was time you—well, began to meet people.'

Rachel felt an unaccountable chill slide down her spine. 'Do you want to go?' she asked jerkily.

'Don't you?' he countered.

Rachel sighed uneasily. 'Will—will there be many people there?'

'A fair number. Twenty-five maybe, or thirty.'

'Thirty!' Rachel swallowed hard. 'I see.'

Jake's hand went to loosen his tie. 'It had to happen sooner or later,' he remarked flatly. 'This is your first real taste of what it's like to be Jake Courtenay's wife.'

Rachel's nails dug into her palms. 'Is that what you think?' She drew an unsteady breath. 'Is that what you *really* think?'

'What do you mean?'

'I think there's more to being a wife than attending

parties with one's husband,' she declared tremulously. 'And my tastes lie in another direction entirely.'

Jake pulled his tie free and unfastened the top buttons of his shirt. 'So,' he said, not looking at her, 'will you come?'

Rachel made a resigned gesture. 'If you want me to.'

'Good.' Jake turned back towards the door. 'It's informal. We'll leave in about an hour.'

Rachel spent at least half that time taking another look at her limited wardrobe. The yellow jersey was all right for an evening at home, but what ought she to wear to an informal dinner party? She tried to remember what Della used to wear on informal occasions, but her tastes had been so much more sophisticated than Rachel's own.

She eventually decided to wear trousers, the black velvet pants and waistcoat she had worn the night Carl took her to the discotheque. That it was also the night when Jake had asked her to marry him she put to the back of her mind, refusing to associate her desire to wear the suit with any faint hopes she might have of arousing Jake's awareness.

When he saw her, however, his eyes did flicker for a second, and then he said quietly: 'Wait—I have something for you.'

He left the living room for a moment, and when he returned he was carrying a soft fur coat over his arm. Rachel viewed the sable skins without enthusiasm, but she turned obediently at his approach so that he could drop the warm garment about her slim shoulders.

'Thank you,' she said stiffly, realising her midi coat would not have stood examination by the kind of friends he had, and his eyes narrowed questioningly.

'Is something wrong?' he queried. 'Don't you like the coat?'

'It's very nice,' she replied politely. 'Shall we go? Or would you prefer I changed the rest of my clothes?'

Jake's lips thinned. 'You look very attractive, as I'm sure you're aware,' he said. 'If the coat doesn't appeal to you, it can be changed.'

'I don't approve of animals being slaughtered for their skins,' she declared primly, picking up her handbag.

'I see.' Jake pulled on his own leather overcoat over his fine mohair suit. 'Well, I'm sorry, but furriers have to make a living, too. Rest assured that the animal from whose skin your coat was made is not an endangered species.'

Rachel shrugged and walked towards the door, waiting, as she had become accustomed to doing, for him to open it for her. He did so, stretching past her to reach the handle, and in so doing making her overwhelmingly aware of the nearness of his hard body. His name broke involuntarily from her lips, and he turned to look at her, his eyes darkening as they rested on the parted softness of her mouth.

Then, with a determined stiffening of his features, he wrenched open the door and the cool breeze from the corridor outside dispersed the moments of intimacy.

It was the first time they had been out together since coming to London, and Rachel settled herself in the seat beside him in the Lamborghini with an irrepressible surge of excitement. Those moments in the apartment before they left had proved to her that in spite of his iron self-control he was not indifferent to her, and sooner or later he would have to give in to the undeniable desire he felt for her.

The Forrests lived in Hampstead, but with the heavy evening traffic it took Rachel and Jake almost three-quarters of an hour to reach their house. There were already a dozen or more cars parked in the drive, and while Jake found a space to leave the Lamborghini, Rachel cast anxious eyes towards the lighted windows of the house. So many people, she thought sickly, and all strangers to her. It was terrifying. Even with Jake at her side she was frightened, and she wished their relationship were not such an oblique one. Sure of his love, she felt she could have faced anything, whereas who knows, there might be women at this party who knew her husband better than she did.

Jake locked the car and took her arm to lead her towards the house. He must have felt her trembling because he looked down at her quickly, and said: 'Don't be nervous. They won't eat you.'

'Won't they?' Rachel felt she was answering all his comments with a question. 'Did these people—well, were they friends of—of Denise's, too?'

Jake's mouth turned down at the corners. 'They knew Denise, yes. She was very—sociable.'

'Were you?' Rachel asked, as they mounted the shallow steps to the porch, and a wry smile touched his lips.

'Not in the way you mean,' he told her dryly, and she was unaccountably reassured.

One ring at the bell brought a black-clad maid to let them in, and within seconds it seemed to Rachel they were surrounded by people. People of all ages, young and old, dressed in formal and informal attire, so that Rachel's velvet suit went unremarked, much to her relief.

Their host and hostess pushed their way through the throng to be introduced to Jake's new wife, and Jon Forrest was unquestionably charming. His wife, Petra, was slightly less friendly, and Rachel guessed she had been a friend of Denise's, and therefore felt a certain amount of loyalty towards Jake's first wife.

But she was introduced to so many people during the course of the next hour that faces began to run together, and names simply refused to stay put. Jake did his best to stay with her, but so many of the women wanted to talk to her about her background, about how she and Jake had met, and when they decided to get married that inevitably they were separated.

The Forrests, it appeared, had no children, and the ground floor of their house had been thrown into one enormous room, but even so, guests still seemed to find it necessary to sit on the open-tread stairs. There was a bar, and a plentiful supply of drinks, and long buffet tables providing food for anyone who felt hungry.

Rachel, who had not eaten a thing since lunch time, and then only a light salad, found time to swallow several canapés, some sandwiches, and a fruit salad, remembering only too well what too much alcohol could do to an empty stomach. There were steaks simmering on an indoor barbecue for those who wanted them, but lots of the guests seemed quite content to drink their way through the evening.

Music emanated from speakers set at the four corners of the room, and several of the younger guests were dancing to the rhythmic beat of drums. At the other extreme, Jon Forrest was seated at the baby grand strumming out popular melodies to a group of his contemporaries who joined in the choruses. At times the noise was terrific, and to Rachel, accustomed to the quiet conservatism of the hotels Della frequented, it was all rather loud and nerve-racking.

Escaping from a young man who had asked her to dance, after introducing himself as a cousin of Petra's, she sought the comparative peace of the basement cloak-room, and going into one of the toilets to avoid the curious stares of its other occupants, she leaned her forehead wearily against the cool tiling of the wall. Within a few minutes the room had emptied and the silence was as restoring as a benediction. She remained where she was for as long as she dared, and then, just as she was about to emerge, she heard voices as the outer door opened to admit two girls. They were laughing together as they entered, and Rachel's hand faltered at the bolt. Perhaps if she waited a moment she would be able to make her exit unobserved, she thought, not immediately aware that she was in the position of an eavesdropper. Then one of the girls spoke, and her words caused Rachel to freeze into immobility.

'She's awfully young, isn't she? I mean, after the women Jake's known, you'd have expected him to marry someone a little more—sophisticated.'

The other girl sounded less convinced. 'Well, we all know what a bitch Denise was. Maybe he decided not to make the same mistakes again.'

'Ah, but have you heard? Princess Denise is a widow, no less! Old Vittorio couldn't stand the pace, apparently. Anyway, she's on the loose again, and what's the betting she'll make a beeline for London?'

'To see Jake, you mean?'

'Who else? You know she never really cared about anyone else. Jake refused to be at her beck and call every minute of the day and night, and she decided to teach him a lesson, I guess. It didn't work out quite the way she expected.'

'His breakdown?'

'Well, she must have had something to do with it,

mustn't she? After she left, Jake buried himself in his work, and look what happened!'

Rachel's throat felt dry. She wished with all her heart that she had made her presence known before this conversation began. Now she was obliged to go on listening to things she would so much rather not have heard.

'And she's a widow now, you say?'

'Yes.' The other girl lowered her voice slightly. 'I did wonder whether that might not be why Jake got himself married so precipitately. I mean, he must know Denise will want to see him again, and how galling it will be for her to find that he's married now.'

'I see what you mean.'

There were a few moments' silence when Rachel thought with bated breath that she had been discovered. But then two other doors opened and closed, and with fumbling ineptitude she let herself out of her self-imposed prison.

She stood for a few moments in the kitchen before going in to join the party again, oblivious of the activity of the hired staff going on around her, trying to recover some sense of reality. But the things she had overheard were still ringing in her head, and alongside them came the thought that perhaps they were right. Perhaps Jake had married her to thwart any thoughts his first wife might have of taking up where she had left off. Perhaps his protestations of protecting her were merely intended to protect himself, and the reason their marriage had not been consummated might well be because *he* might want to annul it at some later date. He might even *want* Denise back again, but he intended that she should suffer first.

It was all so unreal somehow; not least her own relationship to the man she had married, and yet who was not her husband in the true sense of the word.

CHAPTER NINE

ON UNWILLING FEET she made her way back to the noisy crowd thronging the living rooms of the house, and the first person she encountered as she stepped through the door was her husband. Jake's face was taut with anger, and he caught her arm roughly when he saw her, wrenching her towards him. At any other time she would have welcomed the contact, but right now she was too disturbed.

'Where the devil have you been?' he demanded, his whisky-scented breath fanning her cheeks, dark eyes narrowed between long sooty lashes. 'I've been looking for you for over half an hour!'

Rachel's head swung back dazedly, her hair gold-tipped strands of bright relief against the sombre velvet of her waistcoat. 'I—went to the toilet,' she answered automatically, and then, as the shock of his appearance began to fade, she added stiffly: 'How much longer are we staying?'

His grip on her arm eased slightly. 'Aren't you enjoying yourself?'

Rachel straightened her spine. 'Not particularly. Are you?'

His lips curled. 'I thought you might have welcomed the opportunity to sample a taste of the high life. Jon and Petra's parties are usually very popular.'

Rachel shrugged her slim shoulders, looking down pointedly at his hand on her arm, and with a similar gesture he let her go, pushing his hands deep into the pockets of his trousers. He glanced over his shoulder at the exuberant crowd behind them, and then drew his dark brows together.

'Do you want to go home?'

Rachel sighed, realising her unwillingness to join in the festivities could be construed in several ways. Did she want Jake to think that she couldn't handle it? In spite of what she had learned she wanted to please him, whatever his motives for marrying her might have been.

'I—well, do you?' she asked lamely, and his nostrils flared with impatience.

'Why are you looking at me like that?' he exclaimed. 'Did I do something wrong? I know I haven't seen much of you this evening, but that hasn't altogether been my fault.' He paused, his look narrowing. 'Or has someone been talking to you? Have my good friends been warning you what a selfish so-and-so I can be?'

His words were so near to the truth that an embarrassing wave of colour swept up from her neck to envelop her face, and he scowled angrily.

'Who's been talking to you?' he demanded. 'Petra? One of the others? Or that weak-chinned cousin of hers I saw you dancing with a while back?'

Rachel sought for composure. 'Why should anyone have been talking to me?' she protested, but the expulsion of Jake's breath revealed his irritation.

'Petra was a close friend of Denise. It's not unlikely that she might feel the need to spread a little malice.'

Rachel stared at him mutely for a few seconds, wondering what it was about this man that aroused such strong emotions inside her. Just standing here looking at him, they might have been alone in the room, and she knew an aching wanton longing to be in his arms. If what those girls had said was true and his first wife did

still care about him, what possible chance had she of
holding him when he did not even permit her to share
his bed? And she wanted to. She wanted to tear the
clothes from him and press herself against him, and feel
the rougher skin of his flesh against hers. And why
shouldn't she, she asked herself bitterly, if she was prepared to suffer the consequences?

'*Rachel*!'

His strangled use of her name brought her to the realisation that she was still staring at him, and the smouldering darkness of his eyes made her shake her head
quickly, dropping her gaze.

'Petra—Petra said nothing,' she denied awkwardly.
'I—well, I'm just not used to—to gatherings of this
kind.'

'Nor am I, believe it or not,' he retorted grimly, and
she noticed a faint slurring of his speech. 'All right. Let's
get out of here.'

The Forrests seemed genuinely sorry that they were
leaving. 'You must come again soon, when there aren't
so many people,' Jon exclaimed gaily, patting Jake's
shoulder. 'But I don't blame you, taking your wife away
while you still can. You're a lucky man.'

Jake's smile was polite. 'I know. And thanks again.'

It was a frosty evening, and Rachel breathed deeply
of the fresh night air. It was so good to be out of the
smoky atmosphere in the house, and away from the all-
pervading noise of human voices raised above the music
from the record-player.

But the sudden chill had a different effect on Jake. He
lurched slightly as they made their way towards where
he had left the Lamborghini, and with a sense of dismay
she realised the unaccustomed amount of alcohol he had
consumed had reacted on him. He swore angrily when

he could not get his key into the lock of the passenger side door, and with a determination she had scarcely known she possessed, she took the keys from him and opened the door herself.

'You'd better get in,' she said firmly. 'I'll drive—if you'll direct me.'

Jake stared at her with difficulty through the shadowy light cast from the house. 'Are you sure I am capable of doing that?' he inquired with sarcasm, but she ignored him and walked round to open the other door.

With a sound of self-disgust, he subsided into the passenger seat, and Rachel levered herself behind the wheel, adjusting the safety harness with hands that were not quite steady.

'I'm sorry,' he said quietly, as she endeavoured to make herself familiar with the controls. 'This has never happened to me before. I guess I thought I could take it. I used to be able to.'

'That's all right.' Rachel wished she felt as confident as she sounded. 'Which way do we go?'

The traffic was not so thick as when they started out, and Rachel negotiated the seemingly never-ending stream of traffic signals without incident. She was forced to swerve now and again to avoid jay-walking pedestrians, making their way home after an evening at the pub, and the occasional dog darted in front of them, but generally speaking she made good time, and within thirty minutes they were surmounting the ramp which led into the underground car park below the apartments.

Jake got out of the car slowly, and regarded her across its low bonnet with reluctant admiration. 'Very good,' he said. 'Most efficient. If I ever need a chauffeur, I shall know where to look, shan't I?'

Rachel, who knew Madigan acted as chauffeur when

necessary, raised her dark eyebrows. Relief at not having damaged the expensive vehicle was going to her head, and she answered recklessly: 'I'd rather be your mistress than your chauffeur, darling!' and saw the way his knuckles stood out whitely against the brown skin of the hand gripping the top of the car door. Without answering her, he slammed it shut, leaving her to lock it while he strode away towards the lifts.

The journey up to the apartment was accomplished in silence and she preceded him into the living room rather awkwardly. A white-railed landing divided the room into its two levels, the whole carpeted in shades of blue and gold. Parker-Knoll loungers and creamy velvet sofas created an oasis of comfort, and beyond, a circular oak dining table and chairs, set by the long windows, gave a magnificent view over the rooftops of London.

A square heavy glass table stood on the hearth before an ornamental stone fireplace, and Rachel moved towards this, picking up a magazine she found there, and flicking through it with obviously nervous movements. She heard Jake close and secure the door behind them, and presently, the tread of his feet on the soft carpet.

She glanced up to find him loosening his coat, and his eyes flickered impatiently away from hers. 'I'm going to bed,' he said abruptly. 'If you want anything else, ring for Mrs Madigan.'

Rachel held the magazine open in her hands, looking at him over the pages. 'She'll be in bed, won't she?' she exclaimed. 'I shouldn't dream of disturbing her at this time of night.' She paused, faint colour entering her cheeks once more. 'Is there anything you need?'

Jake shook his head, and turned away, walking towards the door which led to the hall which in turn gave access to the bedrooms. 'I'll say goodnight, then,' he added briefly, and left the room.

When he had gone, Rachel threw the magazine she was holding down on the table again, and stared impotently towards the door which Jake had just closed behind him. He had gone to bed, just like that, without even waiting for her to go to her own room.

She thrust her hands angrily into her pockets, and as she did so her fingers encountered the soft fur of the sable coat. It was a beautiful coat, she thought reluctantly, running her fingers up over the lapels. So smooth and silky; it had a sensuous appeal. She looked again at the closed door, and then, as if coming to a decision, she walked swiftly towards it.

Her bedroom had white walls, a fluffy white carpet, and a white bedspread; shades of cold virginity, she thought now, with sudden insight. The only relief came in the curtains which were threaded with strands of blue and lilac, and hung from floor to ceiling. The adjoining bathroom continued the design, with tiny blue and lilac roses patterned on the tiles which until now Rachel had found quite charming. But tonight she was disturbed and restless, and time had become her enemy, not her friend, making her fight against the core of practical good sense inside her that told her to forget what she was thinking, and like the ostrich, bury her anxieties.

Turning on the shower, she stripped off all her clothes, dropping them carelessly on to the floor. She deliberately ran the water cold, and bundling her hair inside a cap, stepped under the chilling spray. But the invigorating globules were like needles against her skin, so that when she turned off the water and began to dry herself, sensuous warmth flooded her body.

She tugged off the shower cap and gathering up her

clothes, walked naked into the bedroom. She dumped most of the things unceremoniously on to a chair, but she retained her hold on the sables, and on impulse put the coat on again. It swung against her bare legs, arousing a not unpleasant tickling sensation, and she twisted and turned before the long mirrors of her wardrobe unit, wrapping the coat closely about her as she had seen models do in fashion shows.

Then, trembling slightly, she turned towards the door again. Dare she go through with it? she asked herself desperately, the tightness of her throat almost choking her. Dare she go to his room and offer herself to him like some woman of pleasure?

She took a few tentative steps across the curling pile of the carpet, and then halted abruptly. What could she say? What excuse could she give for going to his room? To return the coat? No. That wasn't at all plausible— particularly in the circumstances. What, then? Could she pretend to having heard him call? Dare she suggest she had been concerned about him after he had admitted to drinking too much?

It all sounded far too contrived. Jake would never believe her motives were anything other than calculated. But this might be her only chance, she thought despairingly, even if he was not drunk enough to take what she said at its face value. Yet she had not mistaken the involuntary passion she had glimpsed in his eyes down in the car park. He was not indifferent to her, after all; he had never pretended to be. Surely he would not turn her away.

Her lids dropped as other emotions prickled on her skin. How could she contemplate so dispassionately something which mothers had been warning their daughters about for years? She was married, it was true, but

she didn't feel married, and married people didn't behave as she and Jake were behaving. She had given little
actual thought to the culmination of her plans, and now
her eyes opened wide in half-fearful anticipation. What
if she found she couldn't go through with it? What if
she froze up on him as she had heard could sometimes
happen? How humiliating that would be!

Dejectedly, she turned back to face the room again.
What was the use? she thought glumly. She was simply
not up to it. She was not sufficiently sure of herself—or
him—to play the role of seductress.

So intent was she on her own condemnation that she
paid little attention to the first knocking at her door when
it came. It was not until it happened a second time, accompanied by Jake's imperative: 'Rachel!' that she realised what was happening.

Spinning round on her heels, she hurried to the door
and opened it, holding the soft furs closely about her.
Jake was leaning against the wall outside. Only once
before had she seen him without his clothes, and that
was on the first occasion she had visited the Priory, when
she had gone with him to his rooms while he changed.
But tonight he was not wearing a bathrobe, just white
silk pyjama trousers, that hung low on his hips and outlined the dark skin beneath. He must have taken a
shower, too, because his head was damp, and tiny drops
of moisture curled the fine hair covering his chest down
to his navel. She could see the hard bones of his rib-
cage, and the flatness of his stomach, and her senses
tingled expectantly.

Jake surveyed her broodingly for a few moments, and
she was sure he had not missed the fact of her bare legs
below the sable coat. Then he said curtly: 'I'm sorry to
disturb you, but do you have any aspirin? I've got a

lousy headache now, and Mrs Madigan doesn't appear to have provided anything like that.'

'Oh!' Rachel realised she had been holding her breath and expelled it unsteadily. Then she glanced behind her. 'I—I may have. Will you…' She turned to look at him uncertainly. 'Will you come in for a minute?'

Jake hesitated only briefly, and then straightened away from the wall. He stepped into her bedroom with evident reluctance, and Rachel left him to hurry across to where she had dropped her handbag. She knew she had a small bottle of aspirin tablets somewhere, but her fingers were all thumbs, and it wasn't easy, trying to maintain a firm hold on the sable coat.

'You weren't in bed?' he asked, glancing at the untouched pillows, and she shook her head.

'No, I—I'd been taking a shower. Like—like you.'

Jake looked round the room as if reminding himself of its appointments. 'I don't often get headaches. At least, I didn't until recently.'

Rachel looked up, forcing a sympathetic smile. This was her opportunity, a small voice inside her was exhorting. Why didn't she take advantage of it?

But it was no use. As soon as her eyes encountered the cool appraisal of his, she was forced to look away, unable to maintain a matching indifference.

At last she found the tablets, hidden away at the bottom of the bag, and she brought them out triumphantly and showed them to him. 'I thought I had some,' she said, putting down her bag again and holding out the bottle. 'Take them. I can easily get some more.'

'Thanks.' His fingers touched hers lightly as he took the bottle. 'I'll get Mrs Madigan to stock up. Who knows when I might need them again?'

Rachel followed him to the door, her pulses an almost

audible hammering in her ears. The brown expanse of his back was a palpable temptation, and she had to push her hands inside the sleeves of the coat to prevent herself from touching him.

He turned in the open doorway. 'Goodnight again, then.'

His eyes were briefly gentle, and all thought of caution took wings. 'Jake,' she whispered recklessly, her tongue probing her upper lip. 'Jake—don't go!'

She stretched out a hand to grasp his arm, but the hard muscle she touched was taut and unyielding. She looked up at him desperately, willing him to show some compassion, but the gentleness in his expression had dissolved as swiftly as it had appeared. Her spirits reached their lowest ebb when his free hand came to release her clinging fingers.

'Rachel.' His tone was half tolerant, but he shook his head. 'Rachel, be sensible.'

'I don't want to be sensible,' she protested huskily, moving closer to him, and felt the involuntary shudder that passed through him. 'Jake—love me!'

Jake looked wearily towards the ceiling. 'Rachel, let me go. You'll regret this as much as I will in the morning.'

'No, I won't.' She pressed even closer, and stepping back he came up against the door jamb behind him so that the muscles of his legs were tangible even through the thickness of her coat.

The warm scent of her body rose into his nostrils to mingle with the musky scent of his own, and he looked down at her with eyes that revealed the torment he was fighting. 'What are you wearing under this?' he demanded harshly, and almost of their own volition, his hands parted the skins to reveal the rose-tinted flesh beneath.

He stared down at her silently for several seconds, his breath coming more quickly, and then, with an oath, he gathered her yielding body close against him, his hands sliding naturally beneath the weight of the sables.

'Is this what you really want?' he asked thickly, burying his face in the curve of her neck, and she allowed the coat to fall unheeded to the floor as she wound her slim arms around his neck.

'Really, really,' she breathed, and he propelled her inside the door again and slammed it closed with his foot.

It was ecstasy feeling the closeness of their bodies, and when his hands slid down to her hips, pressing her intimately against him, she trembled with a hunger she hardly understood.

'Just hold me there,' she murmured, as his mouth played with hers. 'It feels so good...'

Jake smothered a groan. 'I know something that feels even better,' he said, his tongue stroking her lips apart. 'Shall we go to bed?'

Rachel lay awake, dry-eyed, long after Jake's breathing had become deep and steady. Turned on to her side away from him, she relived the events of the past hour and tried to find some meaning to it all. So what was all the fuss about? she asked herself half resentfully, feeling a deep sense of disappointment at the thought. She could hardly remember what it was that had driven her to act the way she had, or why it had seemed so important at the time.

Yet she had wanted him, to be possessed by him; and she did love him. That much was certain. But she had expected something else. Certainly he had aroused feelings inside her which had made her lose all control for a time, but the *dénouement* had not been an enjoyable experience. Indeed, she had fought him all the way, and the pain she had suffered was still uppermost in her mind.

Still, she was a married woman now, she thought wryly, in every sense of the word, and if what had occurred had pleased him, then she should be content. But she wasn't. Somehow she wanted more; which seemed ridiculous when she was lying here aching in every limb. How could she contemplate another assault upon her body with anything other than aversion? And yet, turning to look at Jake, his lean, intelligent features relaxed in sleep, she knew she would do anything which might bring them closer together, no matter how unpleasant she might find it.

She fell asleep eventually, but she awakened in those dark hours before dawn to the awareness of a heavy weight lying across her. She shifted on to her back and found that Jake had moved to her side of the bed, his face turned into her neck, imprisoning the tawny-gold disorder of her hair, his arm lying across her rib-cage securing her closely into the curve of his stomach.

A curious lethargy enveloped her at the realisation of his nearness, and she stretched sinuously, arching her body as the emotions he had evoked the night before returned to torment her.

Her movements disturbed Jake, and in the half light that filtered through the curtains she saw his eyelids flicker, and the dark lashes sweep upward.

'Rachel?' he murmured, half questioningly, and she nodded and wriggled closer to him.

'I'm sorry,' she confessed softly. 'I woke you,' and

his eyes narrowed as with returning consciousness he became aware of her slender form beside his beneath the silk covers.

'I slept here?' he probed, then, half to himself: 'Of course I did. I remember.' He rolled on to his back, putting both hands to the back of his neck. 'God, I remember!' He turned back on to his side and stared at her anxiously: 'I hurt you. I'm the one who should be sorry.'

'Don't be.' She was eager to reassure him. 'I—I—it was my fault. I asked you to stay. I wanted you to. Please—don't be angry.'

'Angry? God!' His hand touched her almost as if he couldn't prevent himself, sliding up over the fullness of her breast to close around the hollow of her throat. 'I'm not angry—not with you anyway. But this is what happens when a man can't hold his liquor!' he derided himself harshly.

Rachel felt as if he had slapped her. 'I—I see,' she got out chokingly. 'That—that was all it was, was it?'

His mouth hardened. 'Do you think I'd have hurt you otherwise? There are gentler ways of going about it. My God, I must have behaved like an animal!'

Rachel licked her dry lips. 'It doesn't matter—'

'But it does!' He spoke fiercely. 'It should never have happened. But even looking at you now, I could—' He broke off savagely. 'You must have one hell of an opinion of me.'

'It's over...'

'Is it?' His hand moved down again to caress her with increasing insistence. 'What do you know about it?'

Rachel trembled, reaching to stay his hand when it strayed down over her stomach. 'I—I know I'm inexperienced. You told me that before.'

His eyes held hers. 'You don't want me to touch you any more, is that it?'

'Oh, no—*no*!' Rachel shook her head urgently. 'Only you don't have to feel sorry for me just because you took what was rightfully yours to take.'

'Oh, Rachel, *Rachel*!' With a groan, he moved closer to her again, and she could feel the hard length of him stirring against her. 'Do you think that's what I did? Took what was rightfully mine, I mean? I wanted you— I want you now! But this is not the way I planned it...'

'Some—sometimes things don't go—just the way we planned,' stammered Rachel, unable to prevent the trembling sensation that was sweeping over her, and his mouth twisted sensually as he lowered it to hers.

'No, they don't, do they?' he breathed into her mouth, a sound of reluctant urgency escaping him, and her lips opened willingly like the petals of a blossom burned by the heat of the sun...

When Rachel opened her eyes, a watery sun was streaming through the curtains, painting the room in a pastel light. For a brief spell she lay there blinking in the brightness, unwilling to stir, but then consciousness and recollection brought a bemused smile to her lips. She turned her head sideways on the pillow, but she was alone in the big bed, although the tumbled pillows and the masculine tang of the sheets confirmed that Jake had not long left them.

She sighed sleepily, stretching her arms above her head. Her fears and frustrations of the night before seemed far away now when she recalled the events that followed, and the pain and disappointment had been erased by much more satisfying experiences.

In those dark early morning hours, Jake had made

love to her again, and this time she had been as eager as he, prepared to bear anything to stay in his arms. But what had begun with apprehension had turned to perception, and then she had been lost in the demands of her own senses. She had scaled the heights with him, shared the tender aftermath, and learned what loving was all about.

Feeling the sensuous brush of the silk sheets against her breasts, she realised she was naked in the bed, and suppressing the smile which seemed determined to tilt the corners of her mouth, she swung her feet to the floor. What time was it? And where was Jake? Had he left for his office? Had he left her any message? How would she exist through the day until she could be with him again?

It was later than she thought, after ten o'clock, and she went quickly into the bathroom to take a shower. Her toes encountered something hard on the carpet, and bending, she picked up the bottle of aspirin tablets she had given Jake the night before. Her cheeks dimpled. He had not taken any after all...

She was drying herself with a fluffy green bathsheet when there was a knock at her door. Her senses quickening, she called: 'Come in!' and smothered a grimace when Mrs Madigan appeared.

'Good morning, Mrs Courtenay,' she greeted the girl politely, and Rachel couldn't altogether stifle the automatic response she felt towards the name. 'I'm going to the shops now. Is there anything I can get you?'

Rachel pulled the shower cap from her head, and draped the towel sarong-wise under her arms. 'I don't think so, Mrs Madigan, thank you.' She paused. 'Has—did Mr Courtenay leave for the office as usual?'

'He was late,' replied the older woman conversationally. 'Did you enjoy the party, madam?'

'The party?' Rachel looked bewildered for a moment, and then gathered her wits. Of course, Mrs Madigan no doubt thought they had been late back from their visit to the Forrests. 'Oh, well—it was a change,' she concluded at last. Then: 'I'm afraid I'm not much used to parties.'

Mrs Madigan gave a polite smile. 'Nor is Mr Courtenay, madam.' It was unusual for the housekeeper to speak so frankly, but she apparently decided she had said enough for, much to Rachel's disappointment, she went on: 'I've left some coffee percolating on the oven, Mrs Courtenay. I know you don't much care for breakfast, so if there's nothing you need, I'll get along.'

'Y-e-s.' Rachel hesitated. 'Er—Mrs Madigan?'

'Yes?'

'Did—did Mr Courtenay say anything to you? I mean…' She hastened on: 'Did he leave any messages?'

'No, madam. Should he have done?'

Rachel shook her head. 'Oh, no. No. Not really. I—just wondered, that's all.'

'Will that be all, madam?'

'Yes. Yes. Thank you, Mrs Madigan.'

Rachel dressed in jeans and a matching denim shirt, and took her coffee in the kitchen, seated at the polished breakfast bar. Just for a moment Mrs Madigan had revealed she was human after all, but she was too strictly immured in being respectfully impersonal to succumb to a natural desire to gossip. Rachel couldn't help wondering how long the Madigans had worked for Jake, and whether they had known Denise. She had the feeling that there might be some connection between that and Mrs Madigan's attitude.

She was still sitting there, brooding over the past, when the telephone rang. Realising Mrs Madigan wasn't about to answer it, Rachel answered it herself, and gave a gasp of delight when she recognised Jake's voice: 'Rachel? Is that you?'

'Yes, oh, yes!' Rachel cradled the receiver close against her ear. 'Oh, darling, I was just thinking about you…'

There was a moment's silence, and when he spoke again his voice was slightly huskier: 'I want you to have lunch with me. Will you?'

'Will I?' she echoed eagerly. 'Of course I will. Where? And when?'

She guessed he glanced at his watch, and then he said: 'In about an hour, hmm? Twelve o'clock. At Pasticcio's—it's an Italian restaurant off Regent Street. Get a taxi. The driver will know it.'

'All right.' She was breathless. 'I'll be there.'

'Good.'

She knew he was about to ring off, and said foolishly: 'Jake?'

She heard his sigh. 'Yes?'

'Jake—thank you.'

'For what?' He sounded half impatient.

She paused, unable to put into words over a telephone what she really meant. 'Why—for asking me to lunch, of course,' she answered softly, and he uttered a mild oath before ringing off.

CHAPTER TEN

THE NEXT HOUR was spent preparing for the lunch date. For the first time Rachel wished she had taken the trouble to buy herself some clothes with the generous allowance Jake was paying her. Eventually she was obliged to decide on the green corded pants suit which she had worn several times before, but which assumed an extra dimension when teamed with the sable coat.

Mrs Madigan returned before she left the apartment, and concealed any surprise she might have felt when Rachel told her she was having lunch with her husband.

'Will you both be in to dinner this evening, madam?' she inquired, as the girl was making for the door, and Rachel turned thoughtfully, a finger to her lips.

'I think so,' she said slowly, adding with more assurance as pictures of herself and Jake sharing an intimate dinner for two took root in her mind: 'Yes, definitely, Mrs Madigan. But make it something simple, will you? Something we can serve ourselves.'

'Yes, madam.' The housekeeper inclined her head politely, but Rachel guessed she was not as incurious as she pretended to be.

It was one of the busiest times of the day, and she had great difficulty in finding a cab. The commissionaire who vetted the comings and goings in the apartments was busy when she reached street level, and rather than wait for his assistance, she emerged into the cold January air and endeavoured to summon her own transport. But cab after cab went by, all of them busy, and it was after

twelve before she was actually on her way. Buses and
taxis were lined up nose to tail along Oxford Street, and
Rachel's nerves were jumping by the time they turned
into Regent Street. It was after half past twelve! Why
hadn't she had the sense to leave the apartment in plenty
of time?

Pasticcio's opened into a narrow walkway, and the
taxi set her down in Regent Street, only a few yards from
its entrance. She paid the driver too much in her haste
to get inside, and good-humouredly he handed her a
pound back.

'It wasn't worth it, miss,' he told her with a grin. 'But
thanks anyway.'

Rachel's lips twitched, and stuffing the extra pound
note back into her bag, she hurried towards the restaurant. What if Jake wasn't there? she thought anxiously.
What would she do? Go to his office? She knew where
the skyscraper block was where his companies occupied
several floors, but she had never been invited there.

A black-coated waiter opened the door at her approach and smiled benignly. 'Good morning, madame,'
he greeted her politely, and she managed a faint smile
before searching the discreetly-lit room beyond for a familiar face.

'I—er—I'm looking for Mr Courtenay…' she was beginning nervously, when a tall figure emerged from the
shadows. 'Oh, Jake!' she breathed in relief, and he made
brief introductions to Antonio, the head waiter, before
escorting her to the alcove where a table for two was
laid.

'I'm sorry I'm late,' she exclaimed, in a subdued
voice, after the waiter had taken her coat, but Jake just
indicated that she should sit down on the low banquette

and after she had done so joined her, his thigh firm and masculine against hers.

'A drink, sir?'

The waiter was hovering, and Jake glanced sideways at Rachel before deciding. 'Two gin and tonics,' he ordered after a moment, and the waiter bowed and went politely away.

'I...I couldn't get a taxi...' Rachel started to continue her explanations as soon as they were alone, but Jake's mouth silenced her, reminding her of the passionate intimacy they had shared.

'You're here now,' he said when he lifted his head, apparently oblivious of anyone but her, and her limbs melted beneath the warmth of his gaze.

'I... I...' She tried to gather her composure and failed dismally. 'Oh, Jake...I love you...'

'I know you do,' he agreed dryly, humour lifting the corners of his firm mouth. 'And I've just shown you how I feel. But somehow I don't think this conversation is going to be good for our digestion.'

'I'm not hungry,' she exclaimed unsteadily, and he pulled a wry face at her.

'Don't let Antonio hear you say that.' Then: 'Did you sleep late?'

'Till after ten.' She flushed. 'Did you?'

Jake half smiled. 'Well, not that late anyway. But I'll admit I wasn't at my desk much before then.'

Rachel sighed. 'I wish you didn't have to go to your office every day,' she declared ruefully.

'No, well...' Jake was about to say something more when the waiter interrupted him with their drinks, and thanking the man he said they would order later. 'As a matter of fact, I wanted to talk to you about that.'

'About what?' Rachel sipped her gin and tonic absently. It was not an unpleasant taste, but she couldn't honestly say she enjoyed alcohol in any form. Still, as Jake's wife, she supposed she would have to get used to taking an occasional drink, and perhaps familiarity would breed a certain amount of tolerance. Now she put her glass down and smiled encouragingly at him. 'Go on. What do you want to talk about?'

Jake surveyed her with brooding gravity. 'I have to go away, Rachel,' he told her flatly. 'Tomorrow.'

'Away?' Rachel stared at him in dismay. 'Where?'

'California, as it happens,' he replied, lifting his glass and swallowing half its contents at a gulp. 'San Francisco, to be precise.'

'But—' Rachel's newfound happiness splintered. 'But that's thousands of miles away!' She paused. 'Can I come with you?'

Jake sighed, and turning, gave her a strained moody look. 'I thought of that,' he said. 'As soon as Petrie explained the situation, I thought of that. But it's no good. It wouldn't work. I need all my concentration to get through this deal, and it'll be bloody hard as it is, fighting the jet lag, without the distraction of knowing that you're waiting in the hotel for me.'

Rachel's momentary thrill of possession disappeared beneath a wave of depression. 'But how long will you be away?' she protested.

Jake lifted his shoulders wearily. 'A week—ten days at most. It's the Pearman deal that I was handling before I became ill.'

Rachel pressed her lips together. 'But isn't there anyone else who could go?' she cried. 'Surely after—after what happened, you ought to be delegating some of your work.'

Jake rubbed the side of his nose. 'Yes. Well, that

thought had occurred to me, too, and once this deal is through, I'm considering shifting some of the burden on to Petrie's shoulders.'

'Petrie?' Rachel frowned.

'Yes. Gordon Petrie. You haven't met him yet, have you? He's a good man. He's practically kept the place going while I've been away. He and my father both.'

'Your father?'

'Oh, yes. It was his company in the beginning, you know.'

'And he reported to you?'

Rachel sounded disapproving, remembering the occasion she had seen the elder Mr Courtenay at the hotel, and Jake smiled. 'No,' he said firmly. 'You should know better than that. But I'm not denying that once I went to stay at the Priory, he was keen enough to hand over the responsibility again.'

Rachel looked at him anxiously. 'But you know what Mr Francis said!'

'Max? He's an old woman. And you're beginning to sound like my mother!'

Rachel drew back, hurt by his apparent insensitivity, and with an exclamation, he grasped both her hands in his, and said urgently: 'Try to see it my way. I have to go to San Francisco. I have to wrap this deal up myself. This is exactly the kind of situation I've tried to warn you about. I only wish—'

He broke off abruptly, releasing her and flinging himself back in his seat, his mouth set in a straight line, and Rachel pressed her palms tightly together. 'You—you wish last night had—had never happened, don't you?' she demanded unsteadily, and he turned to look at her again.

'Yes,' he said violently. 'But not for the reasons you think.'

Rachel shook her head. 'Then tell me...'

Jake raked back his hair with an impatient hand. 'I intended you should know exactly what you were getting into,' he explained roughly. 'These trips—the time I spend at the office: they're my way of life. And I wanted you to appreciate that it's no sinecure before...' He took a deep breath. 'As it is, I've thrust you in at the deep end without even waiting to find out if you can swim!'

'Oh, Jake!' Rachel put a tentative hand on his knee. 'I can swim.' She paused. 'But can you?'

His lips twisted mockingly. 'I shall have to, shan't I?' His hand pressed down over hers. 'At least, for the present. And last night has made it harder for me, too.'

'It has?' Her cheeks flamed.

'Yes.' He lifted her hand to his lips, bestowing a kiss in the hollow of her palm. 'Because now I know what it is I'm giving up.'

'You're really—not sorry?' she whispered, and his mouth drew down at the corners.

'What do you want me to say,' he asked, half humorously. 'How can I tell you I'm sorry for what happened when I know full well it will happen again tonight?'

Rachel caught her breath. 'Oh, Jake...'

'And now I suggest we apply ourselves to the menu,' he remarked, making a determined effort to speak casually. 'What do you want to eat? They serve a particularly good pasta here, and the pâté is actually made from an old Italian recipe that dates back quite a number of years.'

Rachel shook her head. 'You choose. Like I told you, I'm not very hungry.'

Jake regarded her with warm concern. 'Stop thinking about tomorrow and think about today,' he urged. 'A week will soon pass. Then I promise you, it will be some time before I agree to go away again.'

Rachel sighed. 'All right,' she yielded. 'I know I have to get used to this, but...'

'I know. It's too soon after—' He broke off. 'It might interest you to know that this life I lead wasn't my choice at all.'

'No. Your father told me. You would have preferred to work with animals, wouldn't you?'

'Mmm,' Jake nodded. 'If I thought—' He broke off again, but this time Rachel urged him to go on: 'Well...' He hesitated. 'If I thought Petrie could handle it, I'd be tempted to buy a place out in the country, like Max for example, and keep a few animals of our own.' He smiled. 'And only come into the city two—maybe three days in the week.'

Rachel clasped her hands together. 'That would be marvellous!'

He looked surprised. 'You'd like that?'

'I'd love it.'

He frowned. 'But wouldn't you rather live in London? I mean...' He shook his head, 'I know some women would.'

'You mean—Denise,' she ventured daringly. 'I'm not like Denise, Jake.'

He gave a wry grimace. 'You don't have to tell me that.'

'Besides,' Rachel caught her lower lip between her teeth, 'if—if we have children, the country is a so much nicer place for them to play.'

Jake turned towards her, his smile definitely provocative, but then the waiter arrived to take their order and by the time he had gone, the moment's intimacy had passed.

All the same, Rachel wished she had taken the opportunity to tell him what she had overheard at the Forrests' party. It wasn't in her nature to have secrets, and she wanted to tell him herself so that she could see what his reactions were. But blurting out that his first wife was now a widow sounded so obvious somehow, and did she really want him to know she still wasn't sure of him even after last night? If only he had told her he loved her! But that word didn't seem to figure in Jake's vocabulary.

The following morning, Rachel awakened with the ominous awareness of impending doom. It didn't even help to find Jake still sleeping beside her, although her lips twitched when she remembered how little sleep he had had. In a matter of hours, he would be boarding an aircraft which would take him thousands of miles away from her, and on top of everything else there was the awful thought that accidents still happened for no apparent reason.

Looking down on him, Rachel wondered what she would do if anything happened to him now. The idea of losing him was terrifying, and she thought she would rather lose him to another woman than have to go on living knowing he was no longer in the world. Bending her head, she lowered her lips to his, and that fleeting caress was enough to bring his arms around her, pulling her down to him with satisfying urgency.

But, later in the afternoon, sitting with him in the airport lounge, Rachel found it incredibly difficult to maintain a cheerful disposition. The minutes were ticking away with agonising speed, and with people about them she could not tell him how she was feeling.

The final call for his flight brought him to his feet and she schooled herself not to break down. Other wives or girlfriends were saying goodbye to their husbands or lovers, and she had to behave as he would want her to.

'I'll ring you—from the hotel,' he promised, and she heard in the timbre of his voice a reflection of her own feelings. It helped somehow, and she turned her face up to his determinedly.

'Look after yourself,' she murmured, and he squeezed her hand tightly.

'I will. You do the same. And phone Mother if you have any problems.'

'She knows you're going away?'

'Yes. I spoke to Father yesterday morning, as soon as I knew.'

Rachel nodded. 'What did he say?'

Jake grinned. 'Told me I was a fool for leaving you behind.'

'You are!' she declared, just for a moment allowing her real feelings to show.

Jake bent towards her. 'You'll be all right, won't you?'

'Who? Me?' Rachel controlled herself again, and feigned a nonchalance she was far from knowing. 'Of course.'

'Of course.'

A look of bitterness distorted his expression for a moment, and cold fingers touched her heart. 'Don't say it like that!' she cried, and the look disappeared as swiftly as it had come.

'I was just thinking what a fool I was, too,' he told

her swiftly, but she had the distinct feeling he had not been thinking that at all.

His mouth sought hers, and their lips clung together for a moment in time. Then, without another word, he set her free, turning away and striding towards passport control without a backward glance.

Rachel didn't wait to see the huge jet take off. Unable to withstand the surging emotions inside her, she hurried down the stairs and out to where Madigan was waiting for her, climbing into the back of the chauffeur-driven Daimler Jake used on these occasions without saying a word.

Back at the apartment, it was worse, with Jake's personality imprinted on every article she touched. It made her wish she had a mother, someone she could go home to and share her misery with. She even thought of Della without bitterness and the others at the hotel, and she felt a curious longing to go back there among people who knew and possibly cared about her.

She could always go to the Priory, of course, but Sheila Pendlebury was there, and while the older girl had neither said nor done anything to warrant Rachel's dislike of her, hostility was there between them like an unseen presence.

She spent a lonely evening watching television, punctuated by a call from Jake's mother. Mrs Courtenay wanted to assure herself that Rachel was not distressed over Jake's departure, and suggested the very thing her daughter-in-law had most hoped to avoid—that she should come down to Somerset and spend the weekend with them.

'Oh, really—Jake's going to ring me every evening,' she protested, searching desperately for a reason to refuse, but Mrs Courtenay was not easily put off.

'Well, he can ring you here just as easily,' she declared at once, overriding that excuse without effort, 'and I know for a fact that he would feel happier if you were with us.'

'But why?'

Rachel could see no reason why Jake's mother should say that, but Mrs Courtenay was ready for her: 'My dear, I hate to tell you this, but we always felt that one of the main causes for the breakdown of Jake's first marriage was what—went on while he was away.'

Rachel's fingers tightened round the receiver. She was still not used to Mrs Courtenay's habit of confiding unsolicited scraps of information.

'Mrs Courtenay,' she began, only to be interrupted by an urgent injunction not to be so formal: 'Er—well, *Mother*, I—' Rachel stifled a sound of frustration, 'I really don't think what happened between Jake and—and Denise has any bearing on this situation—'

'Oh, but it has!' Jake's mother emphasised strongly. 'We all know what it's like for a young woman alone in a big city. Temptation is always in the way...'

'Not in my way,' declared Rachel firmly, but she was fighting a losing battle.

'I know Charles and I live a very quiet life here,' Mrs Courtenay was going on, 'but we would so love to see you, and no matter what you say, *I* know Jake would be relieved to hear you're safe with us.'

Rachel sighed. 'Well...'

'You'll come?' Mrs Courtenay seized on her weakening immediately. 'Oh, good! Shall we say Thursday—or Friday?'

'I was thinking perhaps—Saturday morning,' conceded Rachel defeatedly, thinking with some relief that it was only a matter of forty-eight hours after all. But Jake's mother's terms were rather different.

'Very well,' she agreed without argument, 'and perhaps Charles and I could run you back on Monday and spend a couple of days at the apartment,' making Rachel's return to London merely an extension of her visit.

'Well, actually,' she began recklessly, without stopping to consider the possible consequences of what she was about to say, 'if I do come down to Hardy Lonsdale, I might go on to Torquay afterwards and spend a couple of days at the hotel, with Della.'

'With Della?' Mrs Courtenay sounded disapproving. 'But I thought—that is, Jake told us that you and she— well, were not exactly soulmates!'

'We're not,' replied Rachel levelly. 'But she was a friend of my mother's, and I think she'd like to know that I'm well and happy.'

In actual fact, she didn't know any such thing, but the idea of having Mrs Courtenay at the apartment until Jake came home didn't bear thinking about. She didn't think she could stand any more unsubtle innuendoes about Denise at this time, and nor did she want Sheila coming to their home on the pretext of seeing Mr Courtenay, leaving traces of her personality in the atmosphere.

'Well, you must do what you want, of course,' Jake's mother was saying now, 'but I shouldn't make any hasty decisions about going to the Tor Court. You may find you'd prefer to stay at the Priory, after all. So...' She paused. 'When is Jake due back?'

'A week tomorrow,' responded Rachel tautly. 'Or sooner if he can manage it.'

'Oh, I shouldn't expect him any sooner, my dear,' Mrs Courtenay declared firmly, with the air of one who knows.

'It's much better to expect the worst, then one can only be pleasantly surprised.'

'Yes.' Rachel longed to put the phone down. 'Well, if that's all...' she added pointedly, and at last her mother-in-law took the hint.

'Of course. I must be going. Charles is waiting for his supper, and it's Dora's night off. Ring me tomorrow and let me know what time you'll be arriving on—Saturday, was it?'

'That's right,' Rachel took a deep breath. 'I'll probably wait and ring Friday, if that's all right with you.'

'Very well. We'll look forward to seeing you. 'Bye, dear.'

'G'bye.'

Rachel replaced the receiver with a definite click, and then stood for a moment with her arms wrapped about herself. Why was it that Jake's mother always chose the most inappropriate moments to confide in her? Did she do it deliberately? Or was she unaware of her lack of tact? Whatever it was, she wished Mrs Courtenay would keep her opinions to herself!

Rachel went to bed about eleven, but she couldn't sleep. She tossed and turned for hours, wondering where Jake was and who he was with, and almost jumped out of her skin in the early morning hours when the phone began to ring. For a horrible moment she imagined it might be the airport authorities ringing to tell her that Jake's plane had crashed, and then she remembered that although it was early morning in London, it was still the evening of the previous day in Los Angeles—and Jake had promised to ring her from his hotel.

She leapt across the bed and seized the phone, speaking with unaccustomed breathlessness: 'Yes? Rachel Courtenay speaking.'

'Rachel!'

'*Jake!*' She sank down weakly on to the side of the bed, ridiculous tears pricking at her eyes. 'Oh, Jake! Where are you?'

'I'm at the airport hotel in Los Angeles,' he told her, his voice sounding far too clear to really be coming all those thousands of miles. 'The time here is around seven-thirty, and everyone's just about to have dinner.'

'Dinner!' Rachel was incredulous. 'But you must be exhausted! How was the flight?'

'Boring,' he responded laconically. 'Hours and hours of unadulterated boredom. I managed to sleep for a while, but like you say, I am pretty tired now.'

'Oh, Jake!' It was stupid, but she couldn't think of anything else to say, and the precious seconds were ticking away. 'I'm so glad you phoned.'

'Are you?' he paused. 'What have you been doing?'

She felt an hysterical sob rising in her throat. 'Nothing,' she declared chokily. 'Nothing—but watch television. Oh, and your mother phoned. She wants me to go down there for the weekend.'

There was a moment's silence before he asked: 'Will you go?'

Rachel sighed. 'Probably.'

'You don't have to, you know.'

'I know. But—' she moved her shoulders defeatedly, realising how impossible it was not to understand how he must feel, 'I think they'd like me to go.'

'I'm sure they would.' Jake sounded convinced of that.

Another silence, then: 'Did I wake you?'

'No.' The sob escaped in a nervous laugh. 'I couldn't sleep.'

'Take a drink,' he advised softly, and her lips trembled helplessly.

'J-Jake!'

'Yes.'

'Hurry home!'

'I don't need you to tell me that,' he answered roughly. 'Right now, I feel like getting on the next plane back to England.'

'When—when do you go to San Francisco?'

'I fly up tomorrow morning. I have a meeting with the Pearman board at two o'clock. I'll try and ring you lunchtime, after I've checked in to my hotel. That way I won't get you out of bed.'

'I don't mind,' she protested, and heard his lazy laugh.

'Okay,' he said. 'That's it, then. I'd better go and get something to eat, otherwise I'm going to be mighty hungry by tomorrow morning.'

Rachel couldn't bear to let him go. 'What's the weather like?' she asked hurriedly, and he told her patiently that the temperature was still bordering on the eighties.

'I can hardly believe it,' she exclaimed, and he allowed her a moment's credulity before making his farewells. 'You will ring tomorrow, won't you?' she asked at last, and he assured her he would, ringing off abruptly as if he, too, could have said more.

Rachel sat for a few minutes regarding the cream receiver after she had replaced it in its cradle. So near, and yet so far, she thought wretchedly. Why were clichés considered trite when they were so true!

CHAPTER ELEVEN

RACHEL DROVE HERSELF down to Hardy Lonsdale on Saturday morning. Jake had said she might use the Lamborghini, but with Madigan's permission she was driving the Daimler, which seemed a more conventional kind of vehicle. It was three days since Jake's departure, and he had contacted her every evening, reducing the miles between them through the medium of the telephone. She had still not got over the thrill of hearing his voice, and half resented the realisation that this evening she might not be alone to receive his call. He had promised to ring her at the Priory for the next two evenings, but she had not yet mentioned that she might go on to Torquay on Monday, refusing to admit to a certain reluctance in doing so. Carl Yates would be at the hotel, and she didn't want Jake to jump to the wrong conclusions. All the same, unless she changed her mind about Jake's parents accompanying her back to London, she was bound to stay at least one night at the Tor Court.

It was lunch time when she arrived at the Priory, and Mrs Courtenay must have been looking for the car, because both Jake's parents came out to greet her as she parked on the forecourt.

'Darling Rachel!' Mrs Courtenay embraced her warmly, and then Mr Courtenay was shaking her hand, leaning forward to bestow a light kiss on her cheek.

'Did you have a good journey?' he asked, taking her case, and Rachel nodded, telling them that the roads had been quiet, as they walked indoors.

'And how are you?' her mother-in-law wanted to know, as they climbed the stairs to the first floor. 'Have you been very lonely?'

Rachel sighed. 'A little,' she conceded reluctantly. 'But yesterday I went to the Francises' house, and met Max's wife, Jean, and I enjoyed that.'

In truth, she had not wanted to accept the consultant's invitation when it was offered, but she was glad now that she had. He had rung in the morning after learning from a mutual acquaintance the previous evening that Jake was away, and suggested that Rachel might enjoy a day in the country. Max himself had collected her before noon, and driven her to his house in Surrey, and she had had a delightful time helping Jean with the new baby, and fighting off the rapturous affection of a huge Old English sheepdog.

'Really?' Mrs Courtenay sounded surprised. 'I didn't know you knew them.'

'Well, I didn't really. Oh, I met Max at the wedding, of course, but I'd never met Jean or the children. They have four children, you know. Three girls and a boy. Paul, he's the eldest, is eight.'

'I see.' Mrs Courtenay sounded disapproving and her husband chuckled.

'Sarah thinks you shouldn't enjoy yourself while Jake's away,' he remarked. 'Thinks you should spend all your time sitting by the telephone, waiting for him to call!'

'That's not true!' Mrs Courtenay was indignant. 'Rachel knows I only want her to be happy. And spending a day with the Francises might be very—suitable.'

'No loose men, you mean,' mocked her husband, leading the way into the drawing room, and Rachel hid her smile.

Deciding it was time for a change of topic, she said: 'I think Jake will need a rest when this trip is over. He sounded awfully tired on the phone last night.'

'Yes, didn't he?'

Mrs Courtenay nodded in agreement, and Rachel raised her eyebrows: 'You've heard from him?'

'Yesterday evening,' supplied Mr Courtenay. 'After he'd rung you.'

'He just wanted to talk about you, actually,' added Mrs Courtenay. 'To ask us to make sure you had a happy weekend.'

Rachel's cheeks were scarlet. 'I see.'

'You're embarrassing the girl, Sarah,' Jake's father reproved. 'Seriously, love, he is concerned about you, and he just wanted to let us know that he hopes to be home by Wednesday.'

Rachel put down her handbag, and sank down on to one of the couches. 'That was—thoughtful of him,' she murmured, but she couldn't help wishing he had rung his parents first.

Sheila joined them as they were having a drink before the meal. She came into the room with her usual assurance, and gave Rachel a confident smile. 'Hello again,' she greeted the younger girl cheerfully. 'How are you?'

'I'm fine, thank you.' Rachel forced a smile. 'Are you?'

'Oh, yes, I'm very well.' Sheila's embracing manner was almost patronising. 'How is Jake?'

'Finding the trip a strain, I think,' Rachel told her quietly. 'It's so soon after...'

Her voice trailed away, and Sheila's lips curled. 'After getting married, do you mean?'

'No!' Rachel was indignant. 'I mean after his illness, of course.'

'I've no doubt it's a combination of both,' remarked Mrs Courtenay with her usual lack of tact, and Jake's father pulled a wry face at her.

'Oh, come on, Sarah! Jake's no weakling! It's going into that office every day that's getting him down. As a matter of fact, he was talking about that last night. Seems he's had this idea of shifting some of the responsibility for Courtenays on to Petrie's shoulders, and only going into the office every other day.'

'But could he do that?' exclaimed his wife, and Rachel too found she was waiting expectantly for Mr Courtenay's answer.

'I guess he could,' Jake's father said at length. 'It's only conceit that makes us think we're indispensable. Besides,' he looked gently at his daughter-in-law, 'I believe he wants to buy a place outside of town, where he can raise a family. Isn't that right, Rachel?'

Rachel's mouth tilted upward. 'I think so,' she admitted shyly, but not even Mrs Courtenay's delighted reception of the news could erase a sudden awareness of the malevolence behind Sheila's smiling countenance.

Lunch for four was served in the small parlour, with Sheila joining them, much to Rachel's dismay. Obviously in the absence of anyone else, Sheila was treated with the casual affection of a daughter of the house, and this showed in a dozen different ways. She was very much at home here, and seemed to find nothing strange about the fact that her own mother had cooked and served the meal.

Afterwards, Mr Courtenay took Rachel down to the stables to show her how the new foal was developing, and for an hour or so, she could relax in the company of someone she really liked. Jake's father was very like his son, they shared the same sense of humour, and for a while she escaped the uneasy uncertainty of her thoughts. It was only when Sam Gordon came looking for him that Mr Courtenay had to excuse himself, and Rachel made her own way back to the house.

Mrs Courtenay wasn't in the drawing room, however, so as she had been told that she was to have the same suite of rooms she had occupied before, Rachel decided to make her way there and unpack. On the way she passed Jake's old room and, on impulse, she opened the door and looked inside, drawing back aghast when she saw Sheila sitting on the bed, looking through a pile of old magazines. Then, common sense telling her that she had as much right to be there as the other girl, she returned Sheila's challenging stare with a degree of confidence she had not known she possessed:

'What are you doing?'

Sheila glanced down at the magazines in her lap. 'Looking for something,' she replied coolly. 'What are you?'

Rachel swallowed her indignation. 'This is my husband's room,' she reminded the other girl levelly.

'Yes.' Sheila sounded unconvinced.

'What are those magazines?' Rachel refused to be intimidated.

Sheila held one up so that she could see the cover. It was a weekly periodical explaining methods of breeding and rearing animals. Rachel frowned.

'Are they Jake's?'

Sheila nodded, and continued flicking through them. 'Mr Courtenay wants me to find an article he remembers seeing in one of them.'

'What about?'

Sheila looked up at her then, her eyes insolently appraising. 'Does it matter? You don't know anything about horses, do you?'

Rachel bit back the retort that sprang to her lips. Instead, she said evenly: 'I'm sure Jake wouldn't mind if you took the magazines along to your own room. There's no need for you to look at them here.'

Sheila's gaze didn't waver. 'Why should I? I like it here.' Rachel had no immediate answer to that, and the other girl went on: 'What's the matter, Rachel? Surely you're not jealous of me just sitting here in Jake's old room while you're making no objections to the company he keeps.'

'I'm not jealous!' declared Rachel, but even to her ears it didn't sound entirely convincing. And then, as the rest of what Sheila had said registered: 'What are you implying? Why should I object to the company Jake keeps?'

'Why indeed?'

Sheila shrugged annoyingly, and resumed flicking through the pages. Rachel could feel her nails digging into the palms of her hands and she told herself severely to calm down. The girl was being deliberately provocative, encouraging her to ask questions, the answers to which might well be ambiguous. Obviously Sheila was not immune from jealousy herself, and as Rachel had expected this she should be prepared for it.

Turning away, she was about to close the door again when Sheila spoke again. 'I should ask Jake how long Denise plans to stay in San Francisco,' she remarked casually. 'Or maybe she's flying back to England with him!'

'Denise!' Rachel couldn't deny the involuntary exclamation, but she felt furious when she saw Sheila's triumphant expression. 'You're wasting your time, Sheila,' she told her coldly. 'You won't split us up by trying to make me jealous of Denise. That was over long ago.'

'Was it?' Sheila quirked an eyebrow. 'Who told you that?'

Rachel refused to give her the satisfaction of answering. 'Excuse me,' she said. 'I have some unpacking to do.'

'You don't believe me, do you?' Sheila observed, putting the magazine she was holding aside. 'About Denise being in California?'

Rachel wasn't sure. She didn't think even Sheila would lie about something like that when it would be so easy to prove her right or wrong. But equally, if it was so, why hadn't Jake told her? She needed time to think this one out, but Sheila wasn't giving her any.

'I can prove it,' the older girl went on. 'The wealthy Princess Denise is not without interest to the sensation-minded public, and since her—husband died a couple of weeks ago, it's rumoured that she plans to come back to England—eventually.'

'I really don't care—' Rachel was beginning, when footsteps sounded behind her, and the rustling skirts heralded the approach of Mrs Courtenay.

'Oh, so there you are,' she exclaimed, including both girls in her greeting. 'Dora's made some tea. Would you like some too, Sheila?'

Sheila's derisive gaze flickered over Rachel's pale face for a moment, but then she shook her head. 'I don't think so, thank you, Mrs Courtenay. I still haven't found that article Mr Courtenay was looking for, so I think I'll carry on for a little longer.'

'Oh! Very well, my dear.' Mrs Courtenay tucked her arm confidingly through Rachel's. 'My daughter-in-law and I will go and take tea together, eh? And she can tell me what it's like being married to my son.'

Rachel wished with all her heart she had never opened Jake's bedroom door. Right now, she might have been in her room, unpacking her clothes, happily anticipating Jake's call. As it was, she was obliged to go with Jake's mother and assume a cheerfulness she was far from feeling, knowing that sooner or later she had to face the fact that maybe Jake had lied to her.

Tea seemed to take an interminable time, particularly as Rachel was not hungry, and couldn't even be tempted by the delicate wafered sandwiches Dora had provided. Mrs Courtenay noticed her abstinence, of course, and drew her own conclusions, but Rachel wished it was only Jake's absence which was making her feel so desperate.

Eventually she reached the seclusion of her own suite and kicking off her shoes, curled her toes luxuriously in the soft pile of the carpet. Perhaps she was jumping to conclusions herself. Just because Denise was in San Francisco did not mean that Jake had gone there to meet her. He might not even know she was there. Like London, San Francisco was a big place, and Jake had business matters to occupy his time. Or did he?

Disgusted by the trend of her thoughts, she walked through the bedroom into the bathroom, and turned on the taps. She would take a bath, relax in the warm water, and let its soothing fragrance dispel the unpleasantness Sheila had been so willing to create.

She dressed for dinner with extra care, determined not to let Sheila see how her malicious gossip had affected her, and was rather disappointed to find only Mr and Mrs Courtenay waiting for her in the drawing room. When she casually asked if they were dining alone,

Jake's mother replied that Frank Evans, the veterinary surgeon, had been invited to join them, providing Mr Courtenay agreed not to spend the whole evening talking shop.

'All I seem to hear these days is horses, horses, horses,' she declared impatiently, and her husband gave Rachel a knowing grin before asking what she would like to drink.

'That's a pretty dress,' he commented, as Rachel moved to join him, and she looked down at the amber-coloured silk with thoughtful eyes.

'Your wife chose it for me,' she conceded, trying to behave naturally, but something in her eyes must have given her away.

'Is something wrong?' he asked in an undertone, as he poured her sherry, and she looked at him ruefully, wishing she dared confide.

'Oh, I don't think your secretary likes me,' she admitted, off-handedly, realising he would recognise any attempt at prevarication, and Mr Courtenay's heavy brows drew together.

'What's she been telling you?' he demanded. 'Just because she's treated more like a daughter than an employee it doesn't give her the right to upset you with her chatter.'

'It was nothing much,' protested Rachel, taking the glass he offered and cradling it between her palms. 'Hmm, something smells good.'

'Sarah told me you didn't eat anything at teatime,' Jake's father persisted. 'She said she found you talking to Sheila, and you looked as pale as a ghost.'

Rachel hadn't realised her mother-in-law could be so perceptive. 'She's exaggerating,' she exclaimed hastily. 'You know, this really is a beautiful room!'

Mr Courtenay regarded her narrowly for several more seconds, and then Mrs Courtenay called: 'Whatever are you two talking about so earnestly? Rachel, come and sit beside me.' She patted the sofa at her side invitingly. 'What time do you think Jake will phone?'

Frank Evans arrived a few minutes later, and the presence of the stocky, middle-aged vet precluded any more awkward questions concerning Sheila Pendlebury. Rachel was conscious of Jake's father's eyes watching her at various times throughout the evening, but conversation was general, and Jake's name was only mentioned once.

When the telephone rang at half past nine, Mr Courtenay went to answer it, returning only a few moments later to tell Rachel it was Jake, and that she could take the call in his study. She was grateful for his thoughtfulness, although for the first time she felt a sense of reluctance about speaking to her husband.

Mr Courtenay showed her into the study, and then went out again, closing the door as she picked up the receiver.

'Hello, Jake!'

'Rachel! So you arrived safely?'

'Yes, I'm here.' She paused. 'How are you?'

'Bearing up.' Was it her imagination, or did he sound restrained somehow? 'How about you?'

'Oh, I'm fine.'

'The parents looking after you?'

'Yes. As per your instructions.' She couldn't resist that small jibe, but before he could take offence at it, she went on hastily: 'How's business?'

'So-so.' There was a moment's silence, and now she felt sure she was not mistaken that Jake had something else on his mind. 'By the way...'

'Yes?'

'I shan't be able to phone you tomorrow. Ralph Pearman's invited me out to his place for the day, being Sunday and all, and I can hardly ask to make a transatlantic phone call from there, can I?'

Rachel's legs gave way and she sank down weakly into the squashy leather chair behind the desk. 'Who—who is Ralph Pearman?' she asked faintly, giving herself time to recover.

Jake sounded surprised. 'You know! I mentioned him the other evening. He's handling the deal here for the organisation.'

'Oh, yes.' Rachel felt slightly sick. 'That Ralph Pearman.'

'Rachel?' He sounded concerned now. 'Rachel, are you all right? Have you been drinking? You sound—sort of—slurred somehow.'

'No, no, I'm fine.' Rachel cleared her throat. 'So you'll phone me Monday? But not here. At—at the hotel.'

'The Tor Court?' His voice was noticeably cooler now. 'Yes, Mother told me what you'd suggested.' He hesitated. 'I'd really rather you went straight back to town.'

Rachel's knuckles hardened. 'Would you?' She straightened her spine. 'Why?' A pause. 'Don't you trust me?'

'Trust you?' Jake sounded taken aback. 'I don't know what you mean.' A moment's silence, then: 'For God's sake, what has my mother been saying to you now?'

'Your mother?' Rachel caught her breath. 'Your mother has nothing to do with it.'

'Hasn't she?' He sounded unconvinced. 'So what makes you think I wouldn't trust you to go to the hotel?'

Rachel's shoulders quivered. 'Trust—trusting has to be a mutual thing...'

'I'd go along with that.'

'Can I trust you?'

'What?' Jake sounded positively staggered, and Rachel wondered if he could do that if he really was seeing Denise. Surely he must know how she would feel about that.

'Your wife—your first wife, Denise—she's in San Francisco, isn't she?' she blurted out wretchedly, and heard his swift intake of breath.

'Who told you?'

'It's true, isn't it?'

Another pregnant pause. 'Yes. It's true.'

Rachel held her breath. 'Have you seen her?'

Jake gave a weary sigh. 'How am I supposed to answer that? Yes, I've seen her. We had lunch together two days ago. Now does that make you happy?'

'No!' Rachel was trembling so badly she almost dropped the phone.

'I thought not.' Jake's voice was flat. 'That's why I didn't tell you.'

'I wish you had.'

'Why?' He sounded half angry now. 'I'd have told you when I got home. Not when I'm half way across the world, incapable of assuring you that having lunch with Denise was not through any choice of mine!'

Rachel drew an unsteady breath. 'You should have told me.'

He swore softly. 'All right, I should have told you. What now?'

Rachel shook her head, then realising he couldn't see her, asked, 'What did she want? Why did you have lunch with her?'

Jake sighed again. 'She's a widow now, did you know that?'

'Did you?'

'Of course.' He sounded impatient. 'Vittorio died six weeks ago.'

Rachel digested this with difficulty. So Jake had known soon after their marriage that his wife was a widow—soon enough to have this marriage annulled if he had wanted it. If only he had told her!

'Anyway,' Jake was going on, 'they spent a lot of time in the States when Vittorio was alive, and they have this house out at Carmel which Denise now wants to sell. She heard I was in town, and asked if I'd lunch with her and give her some advice about her affairs. That's it!'

Rachel breathed more easily. 'I see.'

'And now I'd like to know who started all this,' he muttered grimly. 'Who was it? Mother? Father? I can't think of anyone else who knew who might have spoken to you.'

'It doesn't matter—' Rachel was beginning urgently, when the study door suddenly opened and Mrs Courtenay put her head round.

'I hope I'm not interrupting,' she whispered pointedly, 'but you have had quite a while to yourselves. Do you think I could speak to Jake for a minute?'

Rachel stared at her mother-in-law frustratedly. What could she say? How could she explain that Mrs Courtenay could not have chosen a worse moment to interrupt them?

'I—Jake—' she spoke into the phone. 'Your mother wants to speak to you.'

'Rachel, wait—'

But Mrs Courtenay needed no second bidding, and was already taking the phone from her daughter-in-law's

reluctant hand. Rachel herself hovered in the background, wondering whether she would get another opportunity to speak to Jake, but then, aware of his
mother's half-impatient stare, she felt obliged to leave
the room.

Mr Courtenay met her in the passageway outside, and
made a sound of exasperation. 'Is Sarah on the phone
now?' he asked, and when Rachel nodded, added: 'I told
her not to interrupt you, but you know what mothers are
like!'

Rachel managed a faint smile, but all the while she
was listening for the tell-tale sound of the bell which
would signify the disconnection of the call.

Frank Evans looked up from filling his pipe when they
re-entered the drawing room, and smiled understandingly at Rachel. 'I expect you miss him,' he said, rather
tactlessly, and Rachel could only nod in reply.

She was still standing near the door, her hands twisting nervously together, when Mrs Courtenay came into
the room looking put out. She intercepted Rachel's ex-
pectant look, and shook her head with evident annoyance.

'The line went dead,' she declared shortly, destroying
Rachel's hopes with her words. 'I tried to get the call
reconnected, but the operator said there was a fault on
the line, so I had to ring off.'

'I don't know why you had to interfere,' remarked her
husband abruptly. 'Good heavens, woman, you were
only speaking to him last night. What on earth could
you have to say that was so important it wouldn't wait
another week?'

His wife tilted her head. 'I don't have to give you my
reasons!' she retorted. 'But as a matter of fact, I just
wanted to let Jake know that we're looking after Rachel.'

Mr Courtenay smothered an oath. 'I should have thought that was obvious!'

'Oh, please...' Rachel couldn't bear their quarrelling on top of everything else. 'If Jake wants to speak to me again, he'll ring back.' But she wished she felt as confident as she sounded.

The rest of the evening was an anti-climax, and Rachel eventually went to bed at eleven o'clock to cry herself to sleep once more.

On Sunday she attended the village church with Mrs Courtenay in the morning, and then, after an early lunch, Mr Courtenay took them for a drive down to the coast. It was still cold, but the sun was shining as it had the previous day, and Rachel's spirits rose a little. Jake would be home in three days, and soon this past week would be just a rather uneasy memory.

'Are you going down to Torquay tomorrow?' asked Mrs Courtenay that evening, as they sat by the fire after dinner, and Rachel glanced at her doubtfully.

'I—well, no, I don't think so,' she conceded, and Mr Courtenay looked up from the chess pieces he was studying.

'You're going straight back to town?' he asked, and she nodded.

'I wish you'd told us sooner,' exclaimed Jake's mother regretfully. 'I mean, you heard me arrange to help the vicar's wife with Tuesday's jumble sale this morning.'

'What has that to do with anything?' asked her husband, and Mrs Courtenay sighed.

'I told Rachel that we might go up to town with her for a few days,' she told him impatiently, but Mr Courtenay just looked annoyed.

'You did what!' he declared grimly. 'Us—go up to

town with Rachel! Don't be ridiculous, woman. I can't
go up to London this week. You know I've got Harrison
coming to have a look at the mare, and Sam wants me
to go to Risford market with him. Besides,' he glanced
understandingly at Rachel, 'do you want the lass to think
we don't trust her? Good lord, you've brought her down
here, don't you think that's enough?'

Mrs Courtenay pursed her lips. 'I might know horses
would come before your own daughter-in-law!' she retorted, and again Rachel interposed herself between
them.

'Really,' she exclaimed, 'he—that is, Jake's father is
right. I'd really rather have a few days alone before Jake
gets back. I—have things to do. I want to do some shopping first of all.' Some new clothes, she thought with
enthusiasm. A new wardrobe to show him she, too, had
a flair for fashion.

'Oh, well, if that's how you feel,' said Mrs Courtenay,
sounding offended, and Rachel sighed.

'Jake will be home on Wednesday,' she said gently.
'It's only a matter of two days.'

'Is it?' Mrs Courtenay looked vaguely uneasy now.
'He didn't say exactly when he'd be home to me.'

'He wouldn't,' said her husband sardonically. 'He'd
be afraid he'd find you on the threshold!'

'Charles!' Mrs Courtenay's cheeks flamed. 'How dare
you say such a thing! I hope I know my place better
than that. You're both the same, you and Jake always
accusing me of things I wouldn't do!'

Mr Courtenay frowned. 'Do I detect a note of anxiety
in your voice?' he demanded. 'What do you mean—
accusing? What has Jake accused you of?'

Suddenly Rachel could guess, and her eyes turned appealingly in Mrs Courtenay's direction. But the older

woman regarded her defensively. 'Jake said you'd found out that Denise was in San Francisco,' she said slowly, and her husband made a sound of exasperation.

'*Sheila*!' he muttered grimly, startling both of them. 'It was Sheila, wasn't it?'

Rachel couldn't deny it, and he shook his head. 'Of course, she was always jealous of Denise when she was here. Why didn't I remember that? But she always behaved so politely to you that I foolishly thought...' He sighed. 'I should have realised, age brings experience. She has more sense now than to show her hand so openly. I'm sorry, Rachel, I should have guessed.'

'What are you talking about, Charles?' fretted Mrs Courtenay, and her husband explained:

'Sheila told Rachel about Denise. Don't you remember yesterday when you told me how pale Rachel was looking? She'd been talking to Sheila then.'

'Oh, that awful girl!' protested Jake's mother. 'How could she do such a thing!'

'Well, it was no secret,' pointed out her husband mildly. 'Jake told me the day before he left that she was staying in California.' He looked at Rachel. 'He wanted to tell you, but he was afraid you might get upset.'

Rachel managed to maintain a composed countenance, but as usual, Mrs Courtenay had to have the last word. 'I can understand how he felt,' she put in, with disruptive candour. 'I mean, Denise was his wife, after all, and she's a widow now. And we all know Jake divorced her, not the other way around.'

'*Sarah*!' Mr Courtenay's tone was threatening, but his wife didn't seem to hear.

'She was a beautiful girl,' she went on reminiscently. 'They made a very handsome couple, everyone said so.

If Jake's breakdown hadn't happened so much later, I'd have said that was the cause.'

Rachel left the Priory at ten o'clock the next morning and arrived back at the apartment soon after one. It was a relief to walk through the empty rooms, re-acquainting herself with her surroundings, knowing she had only herself to please.

Mrs Madigan soon rustled up some lunch for her, and afterwards Rachel rang the Courtenays to let them know she had arrived home safely. Dora answered the call, however, as Mrs Courtenay was visiting the vicarage and Mr Courtenay as usual was down at the stables.

'It's all right,' she assured the housekeeper, when she offered to call Jake's father. 'It's not important. Tell them I'll ring later.'

It was late afternoon when the telephone started ringing, and Rachel hastily put down the book she was reading and went to answer it. She was sure it must be Jake, but when she picked up the receiver, a strange if not entirely unfamiliar voice asked to speak to her.

'This is Rachel Courtenay speaking,' she said, frowning. 'Who's that? Carl? Carl, is that really you?'

A sound from the doorway made her look up and seeing Mrs Madigan she shook her head quickly, putting her hand over the receiver. 'It's all right,' she said. 'I can handle it,' and the housekeeper went quietly away.

'Rachel?' Carl's voice sounded urgent, and she removed her hand and said: 'What is it, Carl? Why are you ringing? Are you in London?'

'No,' Carl was abrupt: 'I'm at the hotel. I'm ringing you because I'm afraid I have some—bad news.'

'Bad news!' Immediately Rachel's fears were for Jake. 'Wh-what bad news?'

'It's Mrs Faulkner-Stewart,' replied Carl quietly. 'I'm afraid she had a heart attack and died on Saturday.'

'What?' Rachel was shocked and horrified. 'But she wasn't old!'

'Forty-five, to be precise,' said Carl heavily. 'It was a shock for us, believe me. She was playing cards with the others as usual, when she complained of feeling sick.' He paused. 'It was all over in a few minutes.'

'But what did the doctors say it was?' Rachel could hardly take it in.

'Coronary thrombosis.' Carl sighed. 'She was very unfit, as you know, and—well, who knows why these things happen?'

Rachel shook her head disbelievingly. 'So when is the funeral?'

'Tomorrow. That's what I was ringing you about. I tried to reach you on Saturday, but your housekeeper told me you were away for the weekend.'

'If only you'd asked where!' exclaimed Rachel, wondering with hindsight whether her desire to visit the hotel had in some way been connected with Della's illness. Now it was too late—but she would attend the funeral. 'I was spending the weekend with the Courtenays at Hardy Lonsdale.'

Carl made an exclamation of regret. 'If only I'd known! I suppose it's too far for you—'

'Oh, no.' Rachel was adamant. 'I'll come down. If I leave right away, I should be there before supper.'

'Now wait a minute...' Carl was less enthusiastic. 'It's freezing hard down here tonight, and after the thaw of the last few days, the roads are pretty slippery.'

'I'll drive carefully,' said Rachel at once. 'And at least the roads aren't busy at this time of year.' She sighed. 'Thanks for ringing, Carl. I'm glad you told me. It's only right that Della should have someone—of her own at the funeral.'

Mrs Madigan looked dismayed when Rachel said she was driving south again. 'But it's five o'clock, Mrs Courtenay!' she exclaimed. 'You can't drive down to Devon tonight.'

'I have to,' said Rachel simply, deciding not to go into unnecessary details about her reasons for going. It was nothing to do with the housekeeper after all, and she would be home again tomorrow evening after the funeral was over.

She filled up the petrol tank at the nearest garage, and joined the M3 going west. She picked up the A30 before reaching Salisbury, and drove on feeling the first real twinges of weariness when she saw how far it still was to Bath and Glastonbury. Her eyes were pricking painfully by the time she reached the next village, and finding it to be Melford she realised with a sense of dismay that she had inadvertently got on to the Warminster road. It meant a detour of some twenty and more miles to get back on to the right road again, unless she turned round now and went back the way she had come.

Turning round seemed the lesser of two evils, but she had to go beyond the village to find a suitable spot. Then, in the darkness, she misjudged the turn, and found her back wheels spinning helplessly over the edge of a ditch.

It was the last straw, and she got out of the car half tearfully, staring at the car's predicament in angry frustration. The removal of her weight from the car, however, was sufficient to set it rolling backwards, and there was an ominous crack as it lurched into the muddy water of the ditch.

'Oh, damn, damn!' she muttered miserably to herself. Now what was she going to do?

At least the village wasn't far away, she consoled herself grimly, tugging her overnight case from the back of the car, and locking it securely. Not that anyone could drive it away, she decided, but they might dismantle the radio, or even the engine if they were desperate.

Trudging back along the road towards the village, she had to contend with one or two casually-flung invitations from drivers passing her by, but fortunately no one seriously accosted her, and she reached the only pub Melford boasted some fifteen minutes later.

The landlord was sympathetic when she told her tale. 'We don't usually accommodate any overnight visitors here,' he told her frankly, 'but I've no doubt my missus'll find you a bed for all that.'

'You're very kind.' Rachel felt embarrassed by the interested stares of the bar-patrons who could hear everything they were saying. 'Perhaps in the morning someone could go and tow in my car, and if it's damaged in some way, I wonder if there's a hire car or a taxi I could use to get to Torquay.'

'I'll have a word with Tommy Hastings,' promised the landlord, calling for his wife, and Rachel asked if there was a phone she could use. 'Just that one there,' he replied, indicating a pay-phone hanging on the wall, within sight and sound of his customers, and after a moment's hesitation, Rachel shook her head.

'It's all right,' she said quickly. 'It wasn't important.'

It was good to get to bed that night, even if the mattress was lumpy, and the sheets smelled of mothballs. She had driven more than three hundred miles that day and she was exhausted. She lay for a while worrying about Jake calling her, either at the apartment or at the hotel, and then oblivion claimed her.

Annoyingly, she slept late in the morning, perhaps due to the unsettled nights she had been spending lately, and it was after nine when she came down the rough wooden staircase. The hall which led through to the bar was deserted, but a girl of perhaps sixteen was cleaning out the fireplace in what appeared to be the parlour, and Rachel addressed her from the doorway: 'Will it be all right if I use the phone?'

The girl looked up and then got to her feet. 'You'd be Mrs Courtenay, I suppose,' she said, her plump cheeks radiating a smiling good humour. 'Mum said you were staying the night. Do you want some breakfast? Mum said to get you anything you wanted.'

Rachel smiled in return. 'That's very kind, and I would like some coffee—or tea, if possible. But right now, I'd like to make a call.'

'Of course. Go ahead.' The girl nodded towards the bar. 'There's no one in there right now. Dad's gone into the village to see about your car, and Mum's out back feeding the hens.'

'Thank you.' Rachel paused. 'What's your name?'

'Beth, miss. Elizabeth really. Elizabeth Jopling.'

Rachel nodded. 'Well, I'll make that call now...'

Getting through to the hotel took longer than she expected, mainly because she had to search her pockets and handbag for sufficient change to put into the phone box. But eventually the receptionist answered and she asked to speak to Carl.

'I'm afraid he's not here,' the receptionist replied politely, and Rachel stifled an exclamation before saying: 'He must be!' 'No, madam,' the receptionist continued smoothly. 'I'm afraid he's attending a funeral this morning and won't be back before lunch. Who shall I say has called?'

Rachel slumped against the wall. The funeral was *this morning*, and he had left already! She was never going to make it in time!

'Hello?' The receptionist sounded impatient. 'Hello, are you still there?'

'Yes, I'm still here,' responded Rachel heavily. 'As a matter of fact, I was coming to the funeral myself, but my car's broken down.'

'I see.' The girl sounded a little more understanding now. 'Well, I'm afraid the service is at ten o'clock, so unless you can get here within the next quarter of an hour…'

'No. No, I can't.' Rachel hunched her shoulders. 'Thank you anyway.'

She rang off, replacing the receiver with resigned care. Well, that was that! She had driven all this way for nothing! No doubt Carl thought she had changed her mind about coming, and who could blame him? But what was the point of going on now? Della was dead—and would be buried before she could get there. It had all been an awful fiasco!

Beth appeared as she walked dejectedly back along the passage, and gazed concernedly at her. 'Is something wrong?'

'Sort of.' Rachel shook her head. 'I should have been in Torquay this morning, to attend a funeral, and now it's too late to get there in time.'

'Oh, dear,' Beth sympathised with her. 'Still,' she added brightly, 'the person whose funeral it was won't be hurt by your absence.'

'No.' Rachel forced a faint smile. 'No, you're right there.'

When Mr Jopling came back, Rachel was drinking tea with his wife in the comfortable kitchen of the inn, and trying to respond to Beth's attempts to cheer her.

'We got your car towed in,' he told her cheerfully. 'Half shaft's snapped, but Tommy's already rung the main dealers in Salisbury, and they've got a replacement. He'll go in and get it this morning, if that's what you want.'

'How long will it take to fix?'

'How long?' Mr Jopling frowned. 'Well, Tommy reckons it's at least a four-hour job. Taking into account his travelling time, and the other work he has in hand, I should think he'll have it fixed by tomorrow lunchtime.'

'Tomorrow!' Rachel's spirits drooped. 'I see.'

'Can't be done sooner, I'm afraid,' Mr Jopling assured her, and she agreed that he had done everything he could.

'I suppose I could go into Salisbury today and come back for the car tomorrow,' she mused, and Mr Jopling nodded.

'Of course, you could stay on here if you wanted,' he suggested. 'I mean, I know it's nothing special, but you're welcome to stay if you want to.'

Rachel smiled. 'That's very kind of you, but—'

'I know. You'd rather find an hotel.'

'Not really.' She shook her head. 'I just don't want to put you or your wife to any more inconvenience.'

'It's no trouble,' Mrs Jopling assured her at once. 'The sheets are on the bed now, and one night more or less won't make any difference. Since Beth's two brothers left home, there's only the three of us, and we've plenty of room.'

Rachel didn't see how she could refuse. Besides, she had decided there was no point in going on to Torquay, and it seemed more sensible to stay here until the car was ready than have to return or send Madigan back to pick it up later. But she must get home tomorrow. Jake might be back tomorrow night.

She shivered in anticipation. She would ring Mrs Madigan today and explain the situation so that if Jake rang tonight he would not worry about her.

CHAPTER TWELVE

RACHEL TRIED to ring Mrs Madigan several times that day, but the line was always engaged, and she wondered rather impatiently who the woman could be phoning. She eventually got through in the early evening, and when a man's voice answered, she didn't immediately recognise who it was. The voice was deep, and faintly slurred, and she speculated that perhaps Madigan had taken advantage of his employer's absence to go on a drinking spree.

'Mr Madigan?' she asked. 'Madigan, is that you?'

'*Rachel*!'

The harsh interjection made her nerve-ends tingle, and aware of the handful of interested spectators around her in the bar, she said uncertainly: 'Jake! What are you doing home?'

'Who the hell were you expecting?' The callousness of his tone made her quiver, and she had to steel herself not to show the shocked disbelief that was gripping her. 'Where in God's name are you? And what do you mean by disappearing without leaving any word of your whereabouts?'

'But I did...' she began, then glancing round apprehensively: 'Jake, I can't talk now.'

'What do you mean by that?' There was that curious slur in his tone again. 'Where are you? Who are you with? Yates?'

'No!' Rachel was horrified, aware that his voice must

be audible over the unnaturally hushed silence of the bar. 'Jake, please! Listen to me!'

'No! You listen to me! Either you tell me where you are right now, or you can forget I ever asked, do you understand me?'

Rachel trembled violently. This couldn't really be Jake speaking to her, not like this. Why hadn't he told her he was coming home earlier than he had planned? Why was he behaving as if she had walked out on him? Surely when Mrs Madigan told him she had driven down to Devon, he must have rung the hotel and found out from Carl why she had gone. He was unreasonable! Just because she had not turned up at the Tor Court there was no reason to behave as if she had committed some unforgivable crime. Della was dead! Didn't that mean anything to him? He hadn't liked the woman, she knew, but he must realise that she felt a kind of obligation towards her.

Now she said unsteadily: 'I really don't understand why you're behaving like this. I haven't done anything wrong. I didn't know you were coming home today—'

'Last night, actually,' he put in coldly, but she ignored it.

'—and in any case,' she added, 'I had to come. Carl asked me—'

'He means that much to you?'

Frustration, and the sense of anti-climax she was feeling at having Jake speak to her like this when she had been just longing to be with him again, brought tears of anger to her eyes. 'Oh, Jake, don't be so silly!' she declared, and then the pips sounded, signifying the end of her three minutes. The operator came on the line at once, asking her to put some more coins in the box if she wanted to continue, but Rachel didn't. With a feeling of despair, she replaced the receiver, and then ran swiftly out of the bar before anyone could attempt to sympathise with her.

Her car was ready by eleven o'clock the next morning, and after paying the Joplings more than they asked, she left, eager to get back to London and find out what was going on. It had sleeted a little in the night, and the roads were inclined to be treacherous, so she drove more slowly than usual, chafing at the time she was wasting.

She didn't stop for lunch, and arrived back at the apartment soon after two, to be greeted by an anxious Mrs Madigan.

'Oh, Mrs Courtenay!' she exclaimed with relief. 'There you are! We've all been at sixes and sevens since you left.'

Rachel carried her case into the living room and set it down, looking about her apprehensively. 'Where's my husband?'

'I don't know.' Mrs Madigan rung her hands helplessly, looking totally unlike her normally contained self. 'He went out without having any breakfast, and I haven't seen him since.'

Rachel's legs felt like jelly. 'But I was speaking to him on the phone last night,' she protested. 'He—he didn't say anything to me about going anywhere. Is—is he at the office?'

'No, madam. I rang there. There was a call for him earlier on, you see, and—and the caller wanted to get in touch with him quite urgently. I told—this person that Mr Courtenay wasn't here, and—and they said they'd already rung his office without success. I rang through myself because I thought—well, it was possible that Mr Courtenay might be refusing all calls, but his secretary said he definitely wasn't there.'

Rachel sought a chair and sat down abruptly. 'Then where is he?'

'I really don't know.' Mrs Madigan was obviously worried. 'He—well, he wasn't himself last night. He hasn't been himself since he got back and found you weren't here.'

'But you told him where I was, didn't you?' exclaimed Rachel.

'Yes. I told him you'd driven down to the hotel, in Torquay. And he rang there. But they said you weren't there.'

'I wasn't,' cried Rachel helplessly. 'My car broke down.'

'Well, I believe Mr Courtenay asked for a—Mr Yates, is that right? He wasn't there either, and I'm afraid—' She broke off. 'It's none of my business. I'm sorry.'

'Of course it's your business!' declared Rachel, her heart plummeting at the realisation that Jake hadn't spoken to Carl after all. 'Go on. You believe Jake thought we were together.'

'Well—yes.' Mrs Madigan flushed. 'I'm afraid it's all my fault.'

'Why?' Rachel stared at her.

'It was that call you had that sent you down to Devon, wasn't it?' Rachel nodded, and the housekeeper went on: 'I guessed it was. It was me who told Mr Courtenay that you'd been speaking to someone called—Carl, is that right?'

'Oh, God!' Rachel buried her face in her hands. Slowly she was beginning to understand. She raised her head reluctantly. 'What did he do then?'

'He—he phoned his parents, I think. He told me he'd asked them if you'd said you were going on to Torquay, and his mother had assured him that you'd decided against it.'

'That's true. I had.' Rachel tugged painful fingers through her hair without even noticing it. 'But that was before—' She made a distraught gesture. 'Before—before I married Jake, I worked for my godmother, a Mrs Faulkner-Stewart. She was staying at the hotel in Torquay. She was spending the winter there. Carl—Carl Yates, that is, he's the manager. He rang to tell me that she had a heart attack and died on Saturday. The funeral was yesterday. I—I missed it because I had an accident with the car.'

'Oh, Mrs Courtenay!' Mrs Madigan stared at her in dismay. 'Oh, how dreadful! If only you'd told me!'

'I didn't see any need to,' replied Rachel dully. 'I only intended being away overnight, and Jake wasn't expected back until today.'

'He got back in the early hours of yesterday morning.'

'Yes. So he told me.'

Mrs Madigan put a weary hand to her forehead. 'I don't think he's slept since. When you weren't here, he was frantic.'

'Oh, *God*!' Rachel got unsteadily to her feet and paced anxiously about the room. 'He thought—he probably still thinks I was with Carl!'

'Would you like some coffee, madam?'

Mrs Madigan obviously needed something to do and to please her, Rachel nodded, although food was what she needed to fill the awful empty void inside her. But she knew she couldn't swallow anything but liquids right now, and to fill in the time, she carried her case through to her bedroom. The temptation to enter Jake's room was too strong to dismiss, and she opened his door tentatively, her eyes taking in the tumbled state of the bedroom. The bed had not been slept in, but his soiled clothes and a damp bath towel were strewn on the coverlet, silent witnesses to the shower he must have taken before he left.

Automatically, she gathered the dirty shirt and underwear, resisting the desire to bury her face in them and weep, and pushed them into the linen basket in the bathroom. As she turned away, her eyes fell on the open razor still lying on the shelf above the basin, and a small brown bottle with the lid off that stood ominously beside it.

She picked up the bottle unwillingly. It was empty, but when she tentatively sniffed the neck, a faint odour of geranium leaves assailed her nostrils. She frowned. She had read somewhere that narcotics were derived from certain species of plants and she looked at the label on the bottle. The name of the preparation was unfamiliar, but there was the inevitable warning which was more than familiar. A drug, then. But what drug—and why?

Suddenly she recalled her conversation with Jake the night before. She had thought there was something odd about his voice, and now it seemed possible that he had been under the influence of some barbiturate.

Her lips parted nervelessly. Dear God, barbiturates were killers when combined with alcohol, and Mrs Madigan had said Jake had been frantic. What if he had been drinking? She had seen for herself how alcohol affected him.

Leaving the bedroom, she hurried to the kitchen, almost colliding with Mrs Madigan as she was preparing to carry a tray through to her.

'Was Jake drinking?' she asked, without preamble, and the housekeeper stared at her blankly.

'Drinking?'

'Yes. You know—whisky, beer; alcohol of any kind?'

Mrs Madigan set down the tray again and looked doubtful. 'I don't know. He might have been.' She shook her head. 'Why?'

Rachel was loath to tell her, but she had to tell somebody. She held up the empty bottle. 'This contained some kind of drug. It's empty now.'

'Good heavens!' Mrs Madigan stared at her. 'You don't think—you don't think he might have done something—foolish?'

'Something foolish?' Rachel looked blank herself for a moment, before the full import of what the housekeeper was suggesting occurred to her. Then whole new terrifying possibilities occurred to her. 'You don't think—Oh, *no* Mrs Madigan, I'm sure you're wrong!'

The housekeeper gave a hopeless shrug of her shoulders, and then she said: 'At first I thought—well, I don't know if I ought to tell you this, Mrs Courtenay...'

'Tell me what?' Rachel had no time to stand on ceremony. 'Oh, go on, Mrs Madigan, do! What did you think?'

'It was that call, Mrs Courtenay. The one this morning. From—from Princess Denise!'

'Denise?' Rachel stared at her aghast, and the other woman hurried on:

'Yes.' She looked uncomfortable. 'Mr Courtenay mumbled something about—about her when he found you had gone. I thought—well, when he went out so early, I thought it might have something to do with her then when she rang I knew it hadn't.'

'Denise is in London?' Rachel was stunned.

'Apparently.'

'But how? When?'

'She flew in yesterday, so she said.' Mrs Madigan sighed, then she said quietly: 'You don't have to worry about her, Mrs Courtenay. Mr Courtenay, he's not interested in *her*! My goodness, when they were married there were some goings-on!'

Rachel was trying to absorb what she had heard, and Mrs Madigan, mistaking her silence, added: 'I know it's not my place to say anything, Mrs Courtenay, and I haven't—in the past. But now I think you ought to know that their marriage was not like yours, if you know what I mean. They lived separate lives. They had separate friends. Surely you comprehend my meaning!'

Rachel blinked rapidly. 'I'm beginning to.' Then she mentally shook herself. 'But if Jake's not with Denise, where is he?'

The slamming of the outer door of the apartment caused both of them to start violently, and Rachel's anxious eyes went immediately to the housekeeper's face.

'It's probably Ben,' declared Mrs Madigan quellingly, but Rachel was brushing past her, hurrying through into the living room.

Jake was descending the stairs from the landing when he saw her. He looked pale and tired, and weariness had etched deep lines beside his nose and mouth. For the first time since their marriage he looked older than his years, and Rachel's heart went out to him.

'Oh, Jake!' she breathed tearfully, and forgetting her resentment of the night before, flew across the room and into his arms. Mrs Madigan, behind her, hastily withdrew, but although Jake's arms closed about her briefly, pressing her hard against his taut body, a moment later he had propelled her away from him again, his fingers tight bands around her upper arms. He stared at her unsmilingly for a long minute, and then he said, with suppressed violence:

'Why didn't you tell me that Della was dead?'

Rachel pressed her trembling lips together. 'You didn't give me a chance!'

'You could have left word with Mrs Madigan.'

'I—I didn't think it was necessary.'

'So you'd let me beat Yates to within an inch of his life?'

She gasped. 'You didn't!'

He held her horrified stare for several more agonising seconds, then he shook his head. 'No,' he conceded at last. 'But I might have done.'

'Oh, Jake!' She felt weak with reaction. 'Jake, where have you been? I found that empty bottle of pills in the bathroom, and I thought—' She broke off unsteadily. 'I've been so worried!'

'Have you?' He shrugged. 'Now you know what it's like.' Then he made an impatient gesture. 'The bottle contained amphetamines, that's all. You know—stimulants. To keep me awake. Do you have any idea how I felt?'

'But it wasn't my fault, Jake,' she protested. 'I didn't know you were coming back. Carl...' She faltered at the look in his eyes. 'Carl rang and—and I just had to try to go to Della's funeral. I told Mrs Madigan I was going to the hotel. I thought that would be enough.'

'But you never got there.'

'No. I...' She sighed. 'I tried to turn the car on a narrow road and I ended up in the ditch.'

'So I hear.'

'You hear?'

'Yes.' He straightened, releasing her arms, but she didn't move away from him, just stood there in front of him rubbing the circulation back into her numbed limbs. 'That's one of the places I've been this morning. There—and the Tor Court.'

'You've been to Torquay?'

'Yes. I wanted to know where Yates was yesterday morning when I rang.'

'But how did you know where I was?'

'You forget, you made your call via the operator. I had it traced.'

She gasped. 'I didn't know anyone could do that.'

'They can't. In the normal way.' His lips twisted. 'You've forgotten something else—I do have a little influence in certain areas.'

She shook her head. 'So you spoke to Mr Jopling.'

'Yes. And to Mrs Jopling and their daughter—Beth, isn't it?' Rachel nodded, and he went on: 'They assured me you had spent the last two nights at the Grey Goose.'

His conversation was giving Rachel time to gather her scattered thoughts. 'But,' she recalled unevenly, 'you said that if I didn't tell you where I was...' She halted, flushing. 'Why did you come looking for me?'

Jake gave her an old-fashioned look through narrowed eyes. 'All right,' he said flatly. 'You can have your pound of flesh any time you want it.'

Rachel frowned. 'I don't know what you mean.'

Jake stared at her a moment longer, then he strode savagely across the room to stand staring broodingly down on the rooftops of London. 'Very well,' he said heavily. 'I can't deny it. I came because—well, whatever you'd done, whoever you were with—I had to tell you I couldn't live without you.'

Rachel turned to stare wonderingly at the broad expanse of his leather-covered shoulders presented to her. 'Do—do you mean that?'

He glanced at her then. 'You know I do,' he told her harshly. 'Why else am I telling you so?'

She took an involuntary step towards him. 'But...' She tugged uncertainly at a strand of hair on her shoulder. 'Last night—'

'Last night I was tired and I'd been drinking.' He hunched his back. 'I'd spent almost twenty-four hours trying to find you, and I was half off my head with worry! Mrs Madigan told me that Yates had phoned you, and I couldn't think of any reason why you should have gone haring off down to Devon unless there was something between you two!'

'Oh, Jake, that's crazy!'

'Is it? Is it?' He turned fully to face her. 'I wonder how crazy it would have seemed to you in my condition?'

'Jake, I love you!' she protested. 'I do. I love you. There's never been—there never will be anyone else.'

He covered the space between them, but although she expected him to take her in his arms, he just stood looking at her. 'There's something else you don't know,' he began, but she shook her head.

'I do,' she interposed quickly. 'Denise is in London, I know. She rang here earlier on this morning. Mrs Madigan told me.'

'Denise!' Jake uttered an expletive that Rachel wouldn't have cared to repeat. 'What in hell does Denise have to do with anything?'

'But—I mean—I thought—' Rachel looked confused. 'I thought that was what you meant.'

Jake half closed his eyes. 'Rachel! Rachel! The whereabouts of my ex-wife are of no more interest to me than the whereabouts of Carl Yates to you! All right, I met her in San Francisco. I told you that. But we meet as—individuals; strangers, almost. My God, we only lived together for about a year of the five years we were married. She would tell you that herself if she was here. If she's ringing me now, it's about that house I told you about. I mean, let's be frank, I do know a little more about finance than she does, and her solicitor happens to be a friend of mine. Does that clear it up?'

'You make it sound so—ordinary,' she exclaimed.

'It is ordinary,' he replied with a sigh. 'Rachel, whatever my mother may have said to you, my infatuation with Denise—and that's all it was—was very brief. It never worked. Denise knows that as well as I do. She probably was happier with her ageing prince than she ever was with me. I never fitted into her world, and she sure as hell never fitted into mine.'

'But you—cared about her...'

'I was young and foolish,' he retorted. And then more soberly: 'Perhaps as you are now.'

'Oh, Jake, I'm not foolish. I know what I want.'

Unable to keep away from him any longer, she stepped closer, sliding her arms around his waist and pressing her face against the buttoned fastening on his shirt. For a few moments they remained like that, Jake's body stiff and unyielding against hers, and then his control seemed to snap and with a groan, he gathered her to him. One hard hand turned her face up to his, cupping the fragile hollows of her throat while his mouth played around the edge of hers, coaxing her lips apart before taking passionate possession.

The kiss went on and on, and Rachel was breathless when he finally released her mouth to bury his face in her hair. Her hands were busy, too, unbuttoning his shirt, burrowing against him, secure in the knowledge that he wanted her as much as she wanted him. But eventually, with evident unwillingness, he pushed her away from him, holding her gently between his hands, smiling as her fingers clung to his lapels.

'I still haven't told you,' he said, his voice revealing the disturbed state of his emotions. 'Rachel, Della Faulkner-Stewart left you something in her will.'

'What?' Rachel blinked. 'Oh, Jake!'

He regarded her narrowly for a moment, and then he said: 'Does it make a difference? Della was a wealthy woman, you know. How do you feel about being independent—financially, I mean?'

Rachel shrugged. 'Why should I feel any different?' she asked, sighing. 'But I wish she hadn't done it, though.'

'Why?'

'Oh—well, I don't need it, do I? I mean, there must be other people who would really benefit from suddenly acquiring a nest-egg. Mrs King—or Miss Hardy, for instance. Not me.' She lifted her hand to stroke his cheek. 'I have all I need.'

'Oh, Rachel!' He jerked her towards him urgently, crushing her mouth with his and making her body freely aware of the hardening intimacy of his. 'I'm so glad you said that!'

'Why?' She drew back to look at him, and frowned when she saw he was smiling. 'What is it? Did she leave me sixpence or something?'

'My darling,' he murmured huskily, 'your legacy is downstairs in the car. About fifty pounds of excitable curl and muscle!'

'*Minstrel*!' exclaimed Rachel disbelievingly.

'Minstrel,' agreed Jake dryly. 'Now we really will have to think seriously about buying that house in the country. I'm not having that animal tearing up this place.'

Rachel's laugh was soft. 'You mean I can keep him? You don't mind?'

'Well, let's say I'm inclined to be tolerant of anything if it pleases you,' he told her ruefully. Then, more seriously: 'Rachel, this trip has taught me more than a lesson. I think I needed it. It's proved to me that what I feel about you is no fleeting thing, no casual infatuation, like I felt for Denise. I love you. And believe me, I've never said that to any woman and meant it. That's why I've never said it to you before. I wanted to be sure—absolutely sure. And I am now.' He broke off as she reached up to kiss him, and when he spoke again his voice was husky. 'Rachel, be sure you mean it when you say you love me. I don't think I could stand to lose you now.'

'I mean it,' she told him simply, but sincerely, winding her arms about his neck. 'When you were away, I was only half alive. I want to be with you—and care for you—and have your children...' She touched his cheek tenderly with her lips. 'And I don't care where we live as long as we're together. I don't think that's infatuation, do you?'

Jake hugged her closer. 'I'm only sorry you had to learn about Denise from my mother,' he muttered half impatiently. 'I wanted to tell you myself before I left, but I chickened out at the last minute.'

'Your father explained about that,' she murmured, hoping Mrs Courtenay would forgive her for not bringing Sheila's name into it right now. There would be time enough for that later. 'But you still haven't told me how you came to be home two days earlier than expected.'

Jake smiled. 'Quite simple really. I turned Sunday into

a business meeting instead of a social one. After our conversation on Saturday evening, I just wanted to see you and explain.'

She sighed, pressing her lips to the pulse beating in the hollow of his throat. 'Mmm, I see.' Her tongue appeared provocatively. 'Your heart is pounding, darling, do you know that?'

'Do you blame it?' he demanded huskily, swinging her up into his arms, much of his weariness disappearing already. 'Come on. Let's go and give it something to really pound about, shall we?'

And she had no objections to that.

Harlequin Romance®

Delightful

Affectionate

Romantic

Emotional

Tender

Original

Daring

Riveting

Enchanting

Adventurous

Moving

Harlequin Romance—the
series that has it all!

HROM-G

Harlequin® Historical

From rugged lawmen and
valiant knights to defiant heiresses
and spirited frontierswomen,
Harlequin Historicals will
capture your imagination with
their dramatic scope, passion
and adventure.

Harlequin Historicals…
they're too good to miss!

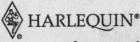
HARLEQUIN®

makes any time special—online...

eHARLEQUIN.com

your romantic life

—Romance 101—
♥ Guides to romance, dating and flirting.

—Dr. Romance—
♥ Get romance advice and tips from our expert, Dr. Romance.

—Recipes for Romance—
♥ How to plan romantic meals for you and your sweetie.

—Daily Love Dose—
♥ Tips on how to keep the romance alive every day.

—Tales from the Heart—
♥ Discuss romantic dilemmas with other members in our Tales from the Heart message board.